THE PLAYER

A ROCK STAR BRATVA ROMANCE

RENEE ROSE

RENEE ROSE ROMANCE

Created with Vellum

PROLOGUE

Nadia

The sound of metallic parts clash in my ears. Cigar smoke fills my nostrils. I hear girls screaming and pleading nearby.

Nadia, look at me. Look here. He slaps my face hard enough to make my head spin. *Open your pretty little Russian mouth, whore.*

"*Nyet...nyet!*"

I jerk awake at the sound of my own voice pleading into the darkness.

I try to move, but I can't—my wrists are immobilized—chained to the bed.

No, wait. They're not. I sit up and rub them to be sure. I'm free. It was just a dream.

Another flashback.

The lamp beside my bed glows because I can't fall asleep in the dark. Worse, if I wake in darkness, I scream until I'm hoarse.

I blink, looking for the cots. For the other girls chained to them, but I'm in my own bed. My own bedroom. Not in

1

the basement of Leon Poval's sofa factory but in our luxury apartment in Chicago. In the bratva building they call the Kremlin.

My brother Adrian and his girlfriend Kat are in the next bedroom. I probably woke them with my cries.

"I'm all right," I call out in Russian, in case they're bracing for my screams.

I climb out of bed and walk to my sewing table to pick up my sketchbook.

Three years ago, when I was a different person altogether, I dreamed of designing wedding gowns. I worked as a seamstress doing alterations in a high-end bridal shop and went to school to study fashion design.

Now, I barely leave the apartment. Agoraphobia keeps me trapped here with my sketchpad full of designs and a sewing machine I never use.

I flip it open to the last drawing I made. Four musicians on a stage. Each wearing punked-out versions of a business suit in black pinstripes and red accents. The jackets have one or both sleeves roughly removed, without a neat hem. One has a lapel missing from the left.

The female lead singer is in tiny shorts with fishnets underneath and a pleated red skirt just on the sides of the shorts. Her red tie is wrapped close around her neck like one of the collars Kat likes to wear.

Then there's her brother, Flynn—the lead guitar player. Tall and dashing. I have him in the jacket missing both sleeves, showing off his shoulders. A red t-shirt underneath—no tie. Black pants with skinny legs. I haven't sketched his face, but my mind conjures it from memory.

Pirate smile. Eyes that crinkle at the edges. A warmth and ease that extends beyond his lanky form.

He's the one thing that lures me out of this building.

Away from the security I derive from living in the fortress of the Russian *mafiya*.

I know his friendliness toward me is just that—a casual amicability he extends to everyone in his sphere. I know he takes a different girl home every week—sometimes two. At the same time.

Flynn is a player. Not the guy for me, and yet I'm drawn to him.

He gives me a reason to try to conquer my PTSD and panic disorder. A reason to leave my room.

I fully expect he'll wreck my heart—that probably can't be helped. But heartache has to be better than the torment of solitude. Or worse—being afraid to feel anything at all.

Flynn

Nadia is having a panic attack.

I'm in the alley behind Rue's Lounge sharing a blunt with my buddies in the band when the stunning young Russian comes flying out the emergency exit door gasping for breath.

She veers quickly around the corner like she doesn't want to be seen.

"I'll see you guys inside." I push off the wall and pass the blunt back to Ty, our drummer. I don't call attention to Nadia, the girl who lives in my sister's building. I'm sure she wants privacy while she tries to get control.

I'm all too familiar with what a panic attack looks like. My mom suffers from anxiety and depression, and I've spent my entire life helping her navigate it. Lightening her moods. Working to make her smile.

I stroll around the corner like I'm still just out for a smoke and find Nadia with her back against the bricks and tears streaming down her face. I don't know her that well.

Not well enough to presume she wants to talk to me right now. Or that I'm any comfort to her.

But I'm incapable of walking away. Not before trying.

Her eyes widen when she sees me, and she gasps harder to catch her breath, doubling over at the waist, her hands resting on her ripped jeans.

I lean my back against the brick wall beside her, so we're side by side. No direct eye contact. No threatening interaction required.

After a moment, she lifts her torso, but she's still unable to breathe. Her face is red and tears leak from the outer corners of her eyes. I can't think of any words to say, so I just take her hand and thread my fingers through hers.

She struggles to inhale for a few moments longer, and then some of the fight drops away, and her arm loosens.

"Hey," I say softly.

She whimpers.

I've been drawn to this girl since she first started coming to see the band. She's gorgeous but in the most understated way—almost like she's hiding. Like she doesn't want anyone to see her. But then she lights up when I talk to her, so I figure maybe she's just shy.

Now I think I understand it better. She has social anxiety.

Which is totally cool. There is no one less daunted by mental health issues than I am.

"I love your new hairstyle." With our hands still joined, I reach up and brush a lock of hair from her brown eyes.

She showed up tonight with copper highlights in her brown hair and her previously long hair cut into a long shaggy bob that frames her heart-shaped face. She's also wearing make-up tonight—another first. Black eyeliner sweeps under her eyes and out toward the outer edges of her brows in a dramatic nod to punk. The upper and lower lids are rimmed and shadowed with gold, copper and bronze that catch the light and make the gold flecks in her eyes pop. She's wearing an open flannel shirt over a pale pink tank top that molds to her breasts.

I purposely don't address the panic attack. I'm not going to ask her what's wrong or if she's okay. I know none of those things will help her move past this moment. She's probably already embarrassed enough that someone has seen her.

"You do?" she chokes out. I hear the relief in her voice that we're not talking about the tears.

"Yeah," I say. "You look great."

She takes her fingers back and wraps her arms around her waist. I push off the wall to face her and adjust the lapels of her black leather jacket, zipping it up because she looks cold. I guess even if you're from Russia, Chicago is too damn cold in February to stand outside for long.

"Do you want a hit?" I ask. I have another blunt in my pocket that I could light up. As soon as I offer, I wish I hadn't.

It feels wrong to offer her weed even though I know marijuana is useful for anxiety. I feel like a reprobate. I have no idea how she feels about partying or drugs or even alcohol for that matter. I've never seen her drink anything but a bottle of water.

Besides, I don't want her to go down that rabbit hole if she's not already in it. I know so many people who've wasted entirely too much of their lives getting stoned— myself included. Nadia seems too fresh and bright for that. She seems pure.

"What?" She looks me in the eyes for the first time since I arrived.

"Never mind," I say. "It was a dumb idea. I have a better one." I catch her hand again and tug her toward the

7

van the band uses to transport our instruments and equipment.

She hesitates, dragging her feet a bit, so I stop to wait. "Are you scared of me?" I am a guy she barely knows trying to pull her to his car in a back alley. It makes sense she'd be reluctant to follow.

But she shakes her head, and the resistance leaves. I pull her to the back of the van where I open the doors. After I crawl inside, I hold my hand out for hers. Her brows go down, but she takes my proffered palm and climbs in. "What are we doing?"

I pull the doors shut and sit cross-legged on the carpeted floor of the van. "It's warmer in here."

She gets comfortable, leaning her back against the side-wall of the van. "Won't your bandmates miss you? I mean, don't you have to go play?"

I shrug. "I'll go back in a minute. For now, it's nice to be away from the crowd. Don't you think?"

Probably understanding that I'm helping her, she tips her head back against the side of the van and lets out a soft sob. A tear streaks down her face.

I keep my mouth shut. This is the art of being with someone in a meltdown. You match their energy. Share the burden. Normalize the moment.

Even though she's crying again, I sense the panic ebb. The tears are the letdown that comes afterward.

"I like my hair, too." Her Russian accent is sexy–I could listen to her all night. "I felt so strong tonight." She swipes at the tears with the back of her hand. "And I want to go to a party with you." When I tilt my head in puzzle-ment, her eyes widen like she wishes she could take the words back. "I mean–you invited me last month, and I wanted to go, but crowds make me hyperventilate. So I've been trying to work on it."

"Yeah," I say like it's all no big deal. Because, truthfully, it isn't. She could freak out or cry all night, and I wouldn't judge. I wouldn't run. I have a capacity for chilling with emotional wreckage.

I let her gather herself in silence for a beat then offer, "We could go to a party tonight."

Her gaze lifts to mine in a sort of shocked wonder. She's wearing a pink-gold lip gloss that makes me want to kiss her pretty bowtie mouth.

"After the show. I already know of at least two parties. We could go to both. You know–try it out. See how you do."

I know she was already writing tonight off as a failure. Maybe she was waiting outside for a ride to go home. But I figure the night is still young. Panic attacks pass. The best thing to do is just move on. Try again. Not make a big deal out of it.

Her full lips part.

"Nadia!" A male voice bellows in the alley.

Only because I hear the panic in his voice–like he's afraid something bad happened to her– do I kick open the back doors to the van and call back, "She's in here!"

I climb out to find the guy I think is her brother striding toward me like he's about to kick my ass.

Nadia follows me out and stands beside me, which makes the guy slow his step. "I'm here, Adrian. I'm fine. It was cold, so we sat in the van for a minute."

He's definitely her brother–there's no mistaking the resemblance. I've seen him in the building a few times. Another one of the lethal-looking tattooed Russian *mafiya* members. I'd be more wary if my sister, Story, wasn't living with one of them.

I guess her boyfriend normalized the mob for me.

His girlfriend runs up behind him and hooks her arm

through his like she's trying to slow his roll. "She's okay. Let's go back in, Adrian."

Adrian doesn't move. He gives me a glower before turning his gaze back on Nadia. "What happened?"

Ugh.

Does this guy not know that bringing it up is only going to bring her down?

"I invited her outside for some fresh air," I lie, looping my arm behind her back like this was some kind of flirtation and not a near-emergency.

He ignores me. "We should go."

I draw Nadia closer. She lets me. She fits nicely by my side, her smaller purple Converse beside my black ones. I like the feel of her against me.

She glances up at me uncertainly. "I-I'm going to stay." She looks back at her brother. "Flynn and I are going to a party after the show."

Adrian's girlfriend's face splits into a smile. "That's great! See? She's fine. Let's—"

"*No.*" Adrian squares off like he's going to fight me if I try to convince him otherwise. I can't tell if he's protective or controlling or both. I'm going to give him the benefit of the doubt and say he's concerned because he knows about his sister's social anxiety, but I don't think making a big deal about it does her any favors. If anything, it reinforces the feedback loop that there's something wrong with her.

It's Nadia who takes charge. She pushes me toward the building, simply walking away from her brother.

"Nadia!" he yells, but he doesn't follow.

I sense both their gazes on our backs as I take Nadia's hand and lead her in through the propped stage entrance door.

Inside, Story is waiting with the rest of the band, her electric guitar looped over one shoulder. She thrusts my guitar at me. "Jesus, Flynn, where in the hell–*oh*." She sees Nadia and chops her own tirade off. "Hey, Nadia. I think Adrian's looking for you."

I shrug off my jacket and toss it over a chair. "He found her," I clip, sliding the guitar strap over my head. I catch Nadia's gaze and see she's starting to turn frantic again. I tip my head toward the stage. "Come here, I want to show you something."

Her body goes rigid. "What?"

"Flynn, we're going on now," Story says with impatience.

I ignore her, stepping close to Nadia, right into her personal space. "Do you trust me?" I meet her gold-flecked eyes with mine.

She locks onto my gaze like I'm a lifeline. Like she's walking on a tightrope, and if she dares to look away, she'll lose her balance and fall.

I shouldn't take offense that her answer isn't immediate. We don't really know each other. We've never even been alone together before those few minutes in the van. She's just a girl who comes to my shows. An acquaintance.

But I know my intentions are good. I know down to my bones that I speak her language. Not Russian. But another one. The emotional one. Or energetic. I may not know anything about her, but I get her completely.

"*Flynn!*" Story hisses over her shoulder as she and the other band members go out on stage. The crowd cheers.

Finally, Nadia gives a tiny nod.

"'Kay. Come here." I send her a smile and take her hand, leading her to the wing of the stage. I yank a chair over and situate it just behind the wing. "Sit here." I point at the seat.

She hesitates, blinking into the stage lights.

"Just sit," I coax.

With faltering steps, she advances and sits in the chair, looking up at me expectantly.

I point toward the stage with a grin. "Best seat in the house," I tell her. "You can see everything on stage in complete privacy."

She cranes her neck around the curtain and darts a look toward the packed house. The air is thick and warm with bodies.

The Storytellers should really be playing bigger venues, but Rue gave us our first job, and we're loath to snub her now. If she decides one day she's sick of the crowds we bring, then we'll move somewhere else. For now, our fans will just have to get here early or buy their tickets in advance because we pack the house and sell out every Saturday night.

"See?" I tilt my head toward the audience. "If you can't see them, they can't see you."

At last, I win one of her rare but beautiful smiles. Like a flower blooming in the snow.

"All right—we are back." Story speaks into the microphone. "We're going to get going with our next set just as soon as my brother gets his butt out here onto the stage."

The crowd cheers. "Flynn! Flynn! Flynn!"

"You okay?" I ask Nadia.

She nods. I see hope shining behind her expression, and it does something odd to my chest.

"Don't go anywhere," I tell her.

Pink stains her cheeks. "I won't."

"Promise?"

"Flynn!" Lake yells from the stage.

I wait for Nadia's answer.

"Promise," she says.

I flash her a smile and jog out to the stage just in time to get hit by three girls' panties at once.

12

———

2

Nadia

Gospodi, girls are throwing their panties at Flynn. He picks a pair up and slingshots it back out into the crowd, which makes the fans—male and female alike—roar in approval. He starts up the riff to one of the Storytellers' original songs.

My heart is still racing, but this time it's not from fear. The mechanical gear sound that starts up when I'm having an attack stopped screeching in my ears.

No, my thrill has everything to do with Flynn Taylor. The guy with a pirate smile who is rapidly overtaking Story's glory as the darling of The Storytellers. The hottest new sound sensation in Chicago. Flynn is becoming the heartthrob every teen girl dreams of. Fortunately, most of them are too young to even get into Rue's. The rest, though...

Let's just say Flynn gets plenty of action.

Which is why I can't decide whether to be thrilled he's taken an interest in me or just write it off because the guy takes an interest in every female in our age range with a pulse.

The band strikes up their second set, and I jiggle my toes to the rhythm and hum along. I know all their songs by heart. I sometimes go down to listen to them practice in the studio in our building. That's where I first met Flynn. I was standing in the hallway waiting to go in and clean the place after they finished. He asked if I was coming to see their show Saturday night.

I'd shocked myself by saying yes.

The first time I tried, I made it to the door and had to leave. The next time, I made it a little longer. I'd come in and sit down with Oleg, Story's boyfriend, the mute bratva enforcer. Once people started coming in, I'd leave. Over the last few months, I've worked my way up to staying for longer and longer periods of time with larger and larger crowds of people.

I think I'm doing so well until something like tonight happens.

I'm not even sure what set me off. There was nothing particularly different about tonight, but when I got up to go to the bathroom, I got jostled by several people, and it set off a full-on panic attack.

It's funny how Flynn didn't seem weirded out to find me crying in the alleyway. I think he was just playing it cool, and I absolutely adore him for that. It was sweet the way he covered for me with Adrian—not that Adrian wouldn't know the truth.

I pull out my phone to text Adrian that I'm backstage, and he can go home without me. It feels wild and daring. Almost as crazy as jumping off a cliff.

He texts back to say he's staying. Obviously, he doesn't believe I'll go through with it.

Am I really going to *a party*?

The idea both thrills and terrifies me. I've been working myself up to this for weeks now. I asked my therapist to prescribe me the anti-anxiety meds she had suggested months ago. I cut and colored my hair. I let my brother's new girlfriend, Kat, do my makeup.

Tonight, when we left the Kremlin, the building that houses Chicago's bratva, I felt on top of the world. Well, not on top of the world–that's going way too far. But I felt strong and bold, like a different person.

The girl in the mirror looked like she could be in a punk rock band like Story. She looked like the kind of girl who could hold her own. The kind no one would mess with.

I may be low-level obsessed with Story. The front person of her own band. The punk rock star with a giant Russian bodyguard for a boyfriend. But maybe that's just because I'm fascinated by everything to do with Flynn. And Story is Flynn's older sister.

I watch him now from the side of the stage. My position lets me be a fly on the wall, and I prefer it so much to being out with the rest of the fans. Back here, I feel safe. I feel like an insider. Especially because Flynn deposited me here.

He made me promise to remain! That thought has my heart racing again.

I take in his tall, lanky form as he performs. He is the epitome of cool–everything a rising star should be. Neatly trimmed beard, a skull cap on his head. His clever fingers dance over the bass guitar strings. He smiles and scowls and performs like a dream.

I watch his shoulders and biceps flex under a faded Radiohead t-shirt as he plays. He's masculine without being threatening. He has that laid-back demeanor that makes it possible for me to breathe when he's around. He makes me forget who I am—which is a good thing.

Because I absolutely hate the skin I live in.

As I watch, a slow pulse starts up between my legs. My breasts get achy. I want him.

I want Flynn Taylor.

I watch the entire set from my vantage point. They play through all their songs, mixing in covers from other bands, as usual. They keep the show fresh for their fans—there's always something new every week.

This week Story pulls out a kick-ass version of Nena's "99 Luftballons." Yes—the German version—and her accent isn't half bad.

When it's over, the band exits the stage, and Oleg, Story's bratva boyfriend who doubles as a bodyguard and sound engineer, comes onstage to pack up the equipment.

The bar hasn't closed yet—they always end a solid thirty minutes before closing time, or else the bouncers can't get people out the door. Tonight they ended even earlier, but no one seems inclined to leave.

In fact, the girls start up a giggled chant, "Flynn! Flynn! Flynn!"

Heat flushes down my neck and arms. I'm not jealous. I'm not. I mean, I have no expectations of Flynn. I'm definitely not reading anything into the fact that he invited me to a party. He probably invited six other girls to go party with him tonight, too.

That thought makes my stomach turn.

Okay, fine. I'm totally jealous. I want Flynn's attention. All of it.

I'm not foolish enough to think I'll get it. I'm shocked he's even noticed I'm alive. I honestly don't know how I even got this far with him. I know I am no threat to any of the girls out there. I'm far too damaged. Barely functioning.

It's been a year since Adrian freed me from the basement of Leon Poval's sofa factory, and the PTSD still has me firmly in its jaws. Some days, I still can't even get out of the apartment.

All I know is Flynn makes me want to try.

"There he is!" One of the young women shouts, pointing in my direction.

I jump to my feet like I'm under fire and find Flynn right behind me, his hands steadying my waist.

It means nothing. He touches everyone, I remind myself, but that doesn't stop the frantic beat of my pulse everywhere.

He spares the young women crowding the edge of the stage a friendly grin and wave, and they instantly take it as an invitation to launch themselves up onto the platform and rush toward us.

When I flinch, he catches my hand, which makes all five of the women barrelling toward us react with comic dismay.

"Are you coming to my party, Flynn?" A gorgeous brunette asks. Her shirt barely contains her ripe breasts, and she has eyebrows to die for.

I don't hate her. Much.

"Yep, we're coming." He nudges me, and her mouth opens in even more visible dismay. She appears semi-drunk, so all of her reactions are exaggerated and obvious.

"Oh. You both are? Well, um, okay. Cool. Who's your friend?"

"Nadia. This is, um…Candice."

"Cadence," she corrects with a scowl.

"Oh right. Totally. Send me the pin for your party?"

Her gaze travels from Flynn to me, and she blinks a

couple times. "Yeah. I mean, yeah. I will." She brushes her hand down his arm, and he doesn't react at all.

I'm already regretting my plan. I can't hang with Flynn. Women like this will be throwing themselves at him all night. What if he decides to hook up with one of them, and I'm suddenly on my own? I need a wingwoman. I wish Kat was single. Which is stupid since I wouldn't know her at all if my brother hadn't brought her home to live with us.

The women walk away.

"Flynn, I don't know about the party," I say.

But just then Adrian appears behind me, like he knew I would fail, and I draw myself up. I can be that woman I saw in the mirror tonight. The chill one with highlights and punk eyeshadow.

"Let's go." Adrian tips his head toward the door.

"No. I'm going to the party."

"I just heard you say you changed your mind," he says in Russian. I guess he's trying to not embarrass me.

"Yeah, and I changed it again," I answer in English. Adrian's right. I need to practice it, or I'll never get fluent.

"I'll take her back to the Kremlin," Flynn tells Adrian.

"No. We will all go to party," Adrian says, which makes Kat bounce in pleasure beside him. She's my age and very social. A party will be right up her alley.

I should be mad, but I'm actually a little relieved. If I freak out, I can duck out with Adrian and Kat.

Flynn splits a look between me and Adrian. "Want to ride with me?"

I nod, a little breathless that he keeps pursuing me this way.

Adrian's upper lip curls as he looks at Flynn. "You touch her, I kill you."

∼

Flynn

Nadia's hand is clammy in mine as we weave through the party. I've already been offered drugs five times. I normally wouldn't be counting. I also normally wouldn't have declined the offers, but something about Nadia's fragility makes me want to stay sober.

Story would be proud of me. She's here at the party with Oleg. The whole Russian contingent came. Probably because no one trusts me with Nadia, which shouldn't irritate the fuck out of me. It's true that I'm not the most reliable guy. I party too much. Sleep around. Shirk responsibilities other than music, and even with that, I suck at the business end of things.

Thank fuck it's actually starting to pay the bills. Ever since we did the music for Skate 32, the Youtube famous skateboard stars, we've really taken off. Our self-produced album gets a lot of downloads, and we're booked two to four nights a week at different venues in town. Story's even talking about us going on a low-budget tour this summer. For the first time in my life, I have more money in my pocket than I need for monthly expenses, and it feels great.

The party builds steam. Someone puts on some music, and at least twenty people crowd in the small apartment.

I don't think this scene is working for Nadia, but I can't really think of a better one.

I don't want to ask her back to my place because that would just end up with us hooking up, which feels wrong. Not because her brother said he'd kill me—and I do believe he'd try. He probably wouldn't even let her leave here with me.

Same as I would've kicked Ty or Lake's asses if they ever tried anything with my sister. I know they're not worthy, and I wouldn't let them even think about trying. And believe me, I know they wanted to. Before she met her giant Russian protector, that is.

I'm not worthy of Nadia, either. I hook up with girls a lot. Okay, all the time. But I don't stick. I don't do relationships. Case in point—Candice-Cadence. Whatever her name is. I had sex with her last week. And it was the second time—a big mistake. One-and-done is a much better policy. Twice is pushing it. Three times, and they think you're married.

But Lake is here, and he's into her, so I'm hoping her interest will shift in that direction. That was the real reason I suggested early in the night that Candice-Cadence host a party. Of course, that was before I knew Nadia was coming out.

Nadia, the beautiful, skittish Russian whose defenses I'm dying to penetrate. I don't know anything about her, but I can tell she's full of potential. There's this flickering glow she tries to hide under hunched shoulders and avoided eye contact. I saw it the first time we met. There's a brilliance that started to show itself tonight in her new haircut and bold eyeliner. And I want to be around when it comes out.

So that means not doing the one-and-done thing with her. Being a friend. Sticking around longer than one night.

So no sex, despite the fact that she's one hundred percent my type. I know I could rock her world and get her to forget all her fears if I just had her underneath me for an hour.

I find a perch on the arm of a couch and tug Nadia to sit in front of me. It's not quite on my lap, but we are nested together, her ass against my angled hips, my arm around her waist. I breathe in her scent, which has warm undertones like butterscotch.

I washed up in the bathroom at Rue's and changed into a clean shirt in the van, but I still wish I'd had a shower. If I were high right now, I'd probably just go be-bop into the bathroom and help myself. But I'm not high, and I'm not leaving Nadia on her own. Not when I can see her back heaving with too-quick breaths. I lean forward, my hand tightening against her belly. "Let's play the story-teller game," I say in her ear.

She turns her head in my direction, and the corners of her mouth lift. "What is that?"

"It's a game my sisters and I used to play when we were bored. An add-on game. Each person adds a new line to the story."

"You have more than one sister?"

"Yes, Dahlia is the baby. She's in college in Wisconsin. The only normal one in the family."

"Okay, let's play."

"I'll start. One time when I was young, I saw a grasshopper."

Nadia gives an embarrassed laugh. "And…since I did not know what a grasshopper was, I ate it."

I chuckle. "But then I learned a grasshopper is an insect, so I quickly spit it back out."

Nadia's face splits into a full smile. She twists to look at me, laughing, her nose wrinkled. "Gross. I'm sorry."

I shake my head dismissively. "Keep going."

"Okay…this grasshopper turned out to be magical."

"It changed into rainbow colors."

"And then it spoke. It said *I will grant you one wish*."

I nudge a lock of Nadia's hair out of her eyes. "And what did you wish for?" I change the game.

She swallows with effort, her lashes fluttering as she meets my eye and then looks down. "I wish to never be afraid again."

My chest aches. "I wish that too–for you."

"What would you wish for yourself?"

I spread my arms and quirk a smile. "To fly!" I say with a grin. "Isn't that everyone's default wish?"

She rolls her eyes, but her laugh is throaty and rich. It makes me want to win it at least one hundred times tonight. To make her laugh and laugh until she forgets all her cares. Everything that caused the pain behind those expressive brown eyes.

"What's up, party people?" Lake hands me and Nadia shot glasses and pours cheap tequila in them.

Nadia looks to me for guidance.

I waver. Loosening her up isn't the worst idea. "Do you like tequila?"

She looks lost. "I have not had?"

Lake tucks the bottle under his arm and waves a salt shaker. "I have salt!"

"What are you, like the tequila fairy?" I ask.

"Yep."

"Where are the limes?" I demand.

Lake shrugs. "No limes. She'll have to kiss your sour pucker for that."

I inwardly wince. For once, I'm not trying to get laid. But it's damn hard to resist when her gaze goes to my lips like she's wondering how I'd measure up.

Well, I am here to show her a good time. One kiss never hurt anyone.

I hold out my palm. "Give me your hand, Nadia."

I'm grateful when she doesn't hesitate. She holds it out to me with a smile. I take her fingers and spread her thumb wide, trying not to think about spreading other parts of her to give access to my tongue. I bring her hand to my lips and suck the webbing between her thumb and forefinger.

She startles and holds her breath, but seems entranced rather than repulsed.

When it's thoroughly wet, I pull back and hold my hand out for the salt shaker. Lake gives it to me with a smirk. He's seen me do this routine at least three hundred times. I don't know why he likes to watch. I guess because I make it into a spectacle, and everyone around gets horny.

It's a party trick.

I shake salt on her moistened skin, then quickly repeat the action to my own thumb pocket. Holding her gaze, I show by example how it's done, slowly sucking the salt off my thumb. I wait until she mimics me, and then we both down our shots at the same time.

"Whew!" She shudders, her mouth screwing up.

"I know. You're supposed to suck a lime now to finish it off. Do you want a kiss?" I'm already reaching for the back of her head, but I would stop and rewind in a heartbeat if she showed any indication of not wanting it.

She nods, her gaze lowering to my lips again. I tug her face to mine and slant my lips over hers, stroking them softly. I tease the seam of her mouth with the tip of my tongue, and she gives me entry, letting me slide my tongue in. She returns the kiss tentatively, letting me lead. I take my time and explore the softness of her mouth, the tangle of our tongues. The lingering salt and tequila taste.

"Hey, I want some of that," Cadence purrs beside us, draping one hand over my shoulder. Lake closes in next to her, giving me a *help-out-a-bro* look.

I guess Cadence is smart. She goes for Nadia, not me, and leans in for a kiss.

"Oh." Nadia's eyes widen, but she lets it happen. Meanwhile, I'm ready to rip Cadence off her if Nadia looks the slightest bit uncomfortable. "Okay," she says when Cadence triumphantly pulls away.

This is another party trick I'm well-acquainted with. It's the free-love thing. Cadence wants me again, but I'm with Nadia and she's with Lake, so she's showing how cool and flexible she is by maneuvering us into a group thing.

My dick is semi-hard because I'm an oversexed male, and the prospect of carnal pleasure is being dangled in front of me, but I would've been cool just hanging with Nadia. No sex. Just making her feel comfortable.

"Come on. Let's go in my bedroom." Cadence speaks only to Nadia, leaving this up to the one person most likely to object.

Nadia shoots me a questioning look.

I lean over and murmur in her ear. "Totally up to you." I mean, I'm not one to turn down a good time. Maybe that's what she's here for.

Cadence picks up her hand and laces her fingers through Nadia's and tugs her toward the bedroom. Nadia follows, so Lake and I close in behind them.

The lights stay off; the door gets shut.

I kiss Nadia because I didn't get enough before. I hear the sounds of clothes being stripped off. Lake's working Cadence. I fill my palm with Nadia's ass, squeezing roughly as I deepen the kiss. Cadence pulls my sleeve toward the bed.

I tow Nadia with me, kissing her the whole way. I get her jacket off and slide my hands under her shirt. She arches against me.

Cadence crawls over to give Nadia another kiss while I cup her breast. She lets out a whimper.

"Oh. Um… where's the bathroom?" Nadia asks.

Cadence laughs throatily. "Down the hall on the left."

"I'll be right back." Nadia slides off the bed and stoops to pick up her jacket.

She slips out the door.

And never comes back.

~

NADIA

Don't panic, don't panic, don't panic.

Everything is fine. I just need to leave. The metallic clanging grows louder inside my skull.

I find Adrian sucking on a beer in the kitchen, standing guard in front of Kat, who sits on a countertop.

The minute he sees me, he knows what's up. He whirls, puts his hands on Kat's waist, and lifts her down. They follow me out of the apartment, down the stairs and out to the street.

I'm not in a full-on panic attack, thank God. Just teetering on the edge of one. My breath is short, the sound of chains rattles in my head.

I guess it's a testament to how much I like Flynn that I even attempted intimacy. I mean, the thought of letting anyone touch me that way ever again usually freaks me out.

For one second there, I was the girl in the mirror. The one who looks confident and tough. When Cadence kissed me, it wasn't scary. Neither was Flynn's kiss. So I figured it might be the perfect opportunity. Try out sex with people who seem safe.

The group thing made it feel safer, initially, although that probably seems strange. The entire time I've crushed on Flynn, I've worried about what would happen if he wanted to have sex, and I couldn't do it. How embarrassing and awful it would be. It seemed like I'd be in the spotlight, and I just knew I wouldn't be able to perform.

So this opportunity–just fooling around at a party with other people–it seemed like less pressure.

And I was turned on. It seemed great.

Until it wasn't.

And now, I just want to clear out of here before Flynn realizes I'm gone.

"Where's the SUV?" I rub my nose, imagining I smell cigar smoke, even though it's not there. I feel the links of chain around my neck tighten. The edge of desperation creeps in.

Adrian presses the fob, and his alarm beeps.

I jog to it and throw open the back door, practically diving in.

Adrian is kind enough not to say I told you so. "Am I going to kill him?" he asks calmly as he climbs behind the wheel after holding the door open for Kat.

"*Nyet.*"

"Are you okay?" Kat twists in her seat to look back at me.

I touch my fingers to the skin around my lips. I still feel the echo of the kiss where Flynn's facial hair tickled me. "Fine. Totally fine. I just... I was done, that's all."

She turns back. "It was fun to go to an American party." Kat is originally from Ukraine but spent the last seven years in England. My brother–who, like me, left his innocence in Russia–kidnapped her there and held her hostage to capture her father but ended up falling in love with her.

Madly in love. They are adorable together. They have wild, kinky sex all day and night, which is part of the reason I'm trying very hard to get better.

I want to move out and give them privacy. Not be so pathetically dependent. Not get triggered by so many things.

I work hard to swallow. "Yes."

Kat turns again. "Flynn is *way* into you." She knows

about my crush on him. She's the one who cut and colored my hair and did my makeup for tonight. Made me feel like I had a chance.

And it seems she was right. Flynn took me to a party. He kissed me. He brought me in a bedroom to make out.

"I don't like him," Adrian interjects.

"You don't have to like him," Kat points out. "It's Nadia's opinion that matters here."

"He lacks honor. I don't trust him. He will hurt you." Adrian meets my gaze in the rearview mirror. "I'm not trying to cockblock. I just don't think he's right guy, Nadia."

"So you *are* trying to cockblock, since he's the one with the cock, and you're blocking him," Kat clarifies.

Adrian makes a grouchy sound in his throat.

"He might be just what I need." I hadn't considered it until this moment, but after tonight's experience, it makes sense.

"What?" Adrian snaps. "Why?"

"I can't be in a relationship. I can barely handle my own life. Mixing it with someone else's would be unwise."

"You want a no-stress guy. No pressure. No commitment. That definitely seems like Flynn," Kat says.

Adrian frowns into the rear-view mirror. "Are you serious?"

"*Da.*"

"You just want…"

"Sex?" Kat fills in.

I shrug. "Maybe."

"No, not maybe. Don't get involved if it's a *maybe*. This guy is a player."

"Yes. It's a *yes*. I think I want sex. I need to get over what happened. To know I can be intimate without freaking. Flynn might be the guy to help me with that."

Adrian makes another disapproving sound. "I'm sure he'd have no problem helping you out with that."

"And you're *not* going to kill him for it," I say firmly.

Wow. I'm already feeling stronger. Making a stand. Demanding what I want. Setting boundaries.

I lean my head back against the seat and rub my lips together remembering the kiss. Flynn's—not Cadence's. I want to remember every detail–how he went in slowly but gradually grew more aggressive. How his masculine scent–like leather and soap–wrapped around me. I want to overwrite my memory banks. For every horrible thing that happened to me, I want a new, shiny memory to take its place.

One with an easy, breezy rock star who makes everything seem possible.

3

Flynn

Sunday, I go to the Kremlin.

Like a dumbass, I never asked Nadia for her number, and I woke up today still feeling like a douche for how things went down last night.

The party was the wrong scene—I'd known that at the time—but the bedroom thing? I don't know how I fucked that one up so badly. I'm good at reading people—especially women. Chalk it up to growing up with two sisters and a mentally unstable mother. I trust the vibes they give off, and I could've sworn Nadia wanted to go in the bedroom. I can tell the difference between when a girl does something because she thinks it's what you want and when she's actually into it herself.

At least, I thought I could tell. So either I fucked up, or she changed her mind, which is cool. I just need to talk to her. Make sure she's okay. Apologize if I'm the asshole.

The building the Chicago bratva call home has security as tight as the actual Kremlin, and the gatekeeper is not a friend. The guy who mans the front desk totally cockblocked me with Nadia last time I invited her to a party. I'm hoping I can bluff my way past him.

But I don't even know which floor Nadia lives on.

Even though the band practices here once a week, I don't have a keycard to use the elevator. I have to park below and then walk around to the front door to be let in. The glass doors–bulletproof, I'm sure–are locked tight. No one is at the front desk.

Fuck.

It's a Sunday morning. I guess they're closed to visitors on Sundays?

I try dialing Story, but she doesn't answer. I text both her and Oleg's phones.

Nothing.

I try banging on the glass door with my knuckles. Not that anyone's there to hear me. I stand outside, loitering for a while, hoping someone will go in and out, but no luck.

Who else do I know in the building? I consider whether I have anyone else's phone number. There's Chelle, the publicist who connected us with Skate 32, the skateboarders. She texted me once. I may have saved her number.

I find her in my contacts as *PR Chelle.*

"Yes!" I murmur to myself.

I send her a text. *Hey, it's Flynn. I'm outside the Kremlin, but there's no one at the front desk. By any chance, could you let me in?*

I don't get a reply, but five minutes later, her boyfriend, one of the blond twins stalks out into the cold. I search my memory bank for his name. Is it Dima? Or Nikolai?

"Nikolai." I hold my hand out to shake his.

He clasps mine but then doesn't let it go. "Text my girlfriend again, and I'll kick your ass."

I try to pull my hand away. He tightens his grip. These bratva guys are serious about their women.

Really serious.

"Fuck, I'm sorry," I say.

Nikolai instantly relaxes his grip, releases my hand, and thumps my shoulder as if to say *no hard feelings*.

"Why are you here?"

I think about going forward with my bluff about having practice, but I know it won't fly. Especially because I didn't bring my guitar. I go with the truth.

"Yeah, well, I need to see Nadia. We went out last night—after the gig—and she left abruptly. I want to make sure everything's okay."

"You went out with Nadia?" Nikolai says it like he doesn't believe me.

"Yeah. After the show."

"Nadia went out with you."

Why does it sound like he doesn't believe me?

"She came to the party with me, but she left with her brother—with Adrian." I never imagined I'd be explaining the whole damn thing just to get through the front door.

Nikolai's expression clears. "Don't worry about it. Nadia often ducks out early. It's not personal."

Now I'm getting impatient. "Yeah, I know she gets panic attacks. I saw her through one earlier in the night. I just need to see her myself, okay?"

Nikolai's eyes narrow. "You have her number?"

Fuck.

"No. I never got it. I wouldn't be here if I had. I mean unless she invited me."

"Yeah, you shouldn't ever be here without an invite."

"Dude, stop busting my balls. I am trying to do the right thing here. I just need to talk to her."

Nikolai grows more relaxed, which makes me want to punch the guy. "Nadia is okay. She has a lot of people here to look after her. You can go home."

"How many people here kissed her last night?" I sound

like a middle schooler. I don't know why I'm trying to make anyone else understand the connection I have with Nadia. I don't need outside approval or recognition.

It gets Nikolai's attention though. He grows alert. "Is that why she left? Did you upset her? You shouldn't have—"

"What the fuck? No, I didn't upset her. I mean—maybe, but she definitely liked the kiss. Kisses, more than one."

I'm an idiot. Why, oh why, do I have to explain this shit to another guy?

"Listen, Flynn." Nikolai takes on a counseling tone. "I know you get a ton of action with the ladies. Just cross Nadia off your list. She's not for you, bro."

Now I'm getting pissed, which isn't like me. I'm an easy-going guy. People underestimate me because I'm laid back. I seem like a slacker or stoner. They mistake my lack of ambition for a lack of intelligence or talent. But for once in my life, I'm not playing it cool.

My hands clench into fists. "You listen, bro." I'm probably going to get my ass kicked here. Nikolai is no less lethal-looking than any of the bratva guys, but I don't care. I've lost patience with this conversation. "She's not on my list. She's a friend, and I need to check in with her. Can you understand that?"

"Huh." Nikolai considers me for a moment, then pulls out his phone and swipes across the screen.

Fuck. Is he requesting ass-kicking assistance? I don't actually know how violent or brutal these guys are. Oleg is a giant teddy bear with Story, but I'm pretty sure he could crush a man's windpipe with two fingers.

Maybe they have a torture room down in the basement. The kind with plastic spread across the floor and a drain in the center for the blood...

Still, I'm holding my ground until I get in.

It seems like an eternity. Nikolai sends and reads a few

texts while I stand there freezing my ass off in the icy February wind that comes straight off the lake.

Finally, he turns and pushes the door open. "Come in."

"Whoa, really? Cool." I drop the aggression and follow him in. He doesn't pause in the reception area, but just heads to the elevators, so I follow him on one. He uses his key card and presses the button for the right floor.

"I don't actually know which apartment Nadia lives in," I admit.

"I'm taking you to the music studio. You'll wait there." The elevator stops, and the doors open. Nikolai walks with me to the practice room Oleg sound-proofed for the Story-tellers and uses the keycard to open the door. I walk in, but he stays out in the hallway. "Go anywhere else in the building, and I'll cut both your hands off."

My brows slam down, and I turn both my palms in consternation. That's...fucked up. How would I play guitar?

"Kidding," he says as he walks away. "Mostly."

"Jesus," I mutter, shrugging out of my leather jacket and tossing it over the back of a chair. The room is carpeted and most of the walls are covered in sound-absorbing molded foam. A large whiteboard covers one wall, so Story can write the playlist or the chords or lyrics to a new song. The studio has a couple of old amps and my acoustic guitar but otherwise is empty because our instruments and equipment are still in the back of the van.

I pick up the acoustic guitar and play a blues riff that's been stuck in my head for days now. It occurs to me that Nikolai didn't say Nadia was coming. Just that I was supposed to wait here. It could be her brother coming to kick my ass.

This is starting to feel like too much.

I set the guitar down and walk to the door, only to open it and find Nadia standing there.

"Oh!" she exclaims. "Hi." She's in an oatmeal sweater that falls off one shoulder and a pair of black leggings with neat rows of rips down the sides.

I resist the urge to gather her in my arms and kiss her senseless. I'd decided not to let things get sexual with Nadia, and they went astray when I abandoned that plan. So back to Plan A. We're friends. *Just. Friends.*

I'm here as her friend to check on her.

"Flynn, I'm sorry," she blurts. "I thought I was going to panic again, and I didn't want to bother or embarrass you."

I shake my head in disbelief. "Bother? No, Nadia, no. It wouldn't be a bother. Or an embarrassment."

She flushes. We're still standing in the doorway to the studio, and it feels like a metaphor. We're teetering between two options—being friends or more than friends.

"What *is* a bother is not having your phone number, so I could make sure I hadn't fucked up." I tip her chin up when she doesn't meet my eye. "Did I fuck up, Nadia? I swear to Christ, I wasn't trying to get into your pants."

Her lips part, and her pupils dilate. "Wh-why not?"

I let out a short bark of laughter and then realize I painted myself into a corner. I don't want to say that she seems like she needs a friend more than a ride on my dick. I don't want to say anything at all that would sound like I think there's something wrong or less-than with her.

I pick up her hand and bring her fingers to my lips. "Because I like you, Nadia."

She pulls her fingers back. "You don't screw the girls you like?"

I grin. "I always like the girls I screw. It's just that I

don't usually continue things longer than that. I don't do relationships. And I wanted to know you for longer."

"Oh." The syllable has a surprised wonder to it, and she sort of falls into my space, so I have no option but to wrap my arms around her. I inhale her sweet butterscotch scent, my dick thickening at her closeness.

Her hands come to my chest, and she looks up at me. "I came down here to ask you to have sex with me."

"What?" This girl confuses the hell out of me.

"Something bad happened to me, Flynn, but being around you makes me feel... better." Her words tumble out in a rush like she wants to say them before she chickens out. Or maybe she wants to continue before I can react. "And everyone's telling me to stay away from you because of what you just said–because you're a player. You don't stick around. But I feel like you might be exactly what I need to get over my...thing."

Something lodges in my throat, making it hard to breathe. I haven't decoded everything she said yet because I got caught on the words, *something bad happened to me.*

It's not social anxiety. It's trauma. No wonder everyone is so protective of her.

And how fucking brave of her to come to me and ask for what she needs.

Who am I to deny her anything at all?

Except I can hear the alarm bells going off. There's a trap in here somewhere. A mistake I'm about to make. I just can't quite figure it out.

"You want to have sex with me to get over your trauma?"

She looks relieved that I understand. "Yes. Just sex, okay? I know you don't want a girlfriend. We could be friends, you know? What do they say here? Friends with benefits?"

I should be overjoyed. This is exactly the kind of scenario that works for me. No pressure, no strings.

Why do I hate it so much?

"You could still have sex with other girls. With Cadence?"

I frown and give a quick shake of my head.

"Right," she says knowingly. "You already had her, didn't you?"

Fuck. This already feels complicated.

She searches my face. "Will you do it?"

All I can do is nod. Of course, I'll do it. I'm incapable of denying this sweet, brave, beautiful girl anything she asks me for.

But the warning bells are still ringing. They're telling me something's wrong about this. Something won't work.

I just can't untangle what it is.

～

NADIA

Awkward.

This is so awkward. I mean, what did I think would happen when I pitch a guy on having friend-sex with me on a Sunday morning in an empty music studio? It's not exactly a romantic location or time.

But then, romance isn't what I'm going for. I don't know exactly how I expect this to work, though.

Flynn studies me like he's trying to figure it out, too. "Want to go get a coffee?" he asks after a beat.

Oh wow. A coffee.

To a normal girl, that would be an easy yes. Coffee with a hot rock 'n roll star. A guy who just agreed to have sex with no strings or expectations.

But I don't do spontaneous, and I don't do outings. The chance for me freaking out is way too high.

But I don't want Flynn to know that. He doesn't know I never leave the building except to see him play. He doesn't know how pervasive my agoraphobia has been. How damaged I am.

I don't want him to know. With him, I feel like I could be another person. Not the old me—that girl is forever gone. But someone new. Someone interesting. Exciting, even.

So I say, "Sure. Yes."

"Do you want to get a jacket?"

I hesitate. If I go back to the apartment, Adrian will be there. He'll doubt I can make it out. Maybe he'll insist on going with me. I'll feel weak and broken—the way I always do around him. It's not his fault. I have been weak and broken. He stopped three suicide attempts the months after he rescued me. He saw me through the most debilitating depression.

But Flynn doesn't know me that way, and I like the me that I imagine Flynn sees. She is light and carefree like him.

She can leave the building without getting upset. Without clinging to the elevator door or the door jam.

But hey, if I can do all those things, I can tell Adrian to give me some space, too—right?

"Yes. Come with me?"

"Sure." He puts his hand on my back and guides me to the elevator. "I had trouble getting to you this morning," he says with his pirate smile. "I didn't know your apartment number. I didn't have your phone number. Nikolai almost kicked my ass for texting his girlfriend to get in the building."

I hold out my hand, still feeling like the bold version of

myself. Like anything is possible and might even not be hard. "Give me your phone."

He hands me his phone, and I text myself with it. "Now you have me." I hand it back with a smile.

"Keep smiling, Peaches." He strokes a thumb across my cheek.

"I don't know this word," I tell him.

"Peaches? The peach is a fruit."

"You are calling me a fruit?"

He gives a casual shrug. Like always, he fills the available space with his presence, but it's not in that powerful, oxygen-stealing way the bratva men do. It's with this casual grace that says he can handle anything you throw at him without batting an eye. Like nothing ruffles this guy. Around him, there's *more* oxygen to breathe, and he makes me feel safe.

"Because you're beautiful. And sweet. Also, you have what we call a peaches-and-cream complexion."

"What?" I touch my cheeks with an embarrassed laugh.

The elevator dings at my floor, and we get off. Flynn follows me off and to my apartment. "Kat and Adrian are still sleeping," I say before I open the door. "Or more likely, in bed not sleeping." I waggle my brows, and Flynn quirks the grin that makes my belly flutter.

"I can wait out here."

I'm relieved by his offer. I'd rather not deal with Adrian if I don't have to, and Flynn's manly voice in the apartment would have my brother out of his bed in a flash.

I really need to move out.

The thought is accompanied by the usual sense of constriction in my lungs, but I picture myself moving in with Flynn, and it completely disappears.

But, of course, I won't be doing that. Flynn doesn't stick around for relationships.

Although he did say he wanted to stick around longer with me. But without sex. And now we're having sex. I mean, we're going to have sex. Ack! I have no idea what it all means. I slip inside, grab my jacket and a knit cap and quickly return, shutting the door softly.

"Oh!" I stop on my way to the elevator. "I didn't get money." I seriously have forgotten how these things work. I haven't been out in so long. Never in America. Not without clinging to Adrian and begging him to take me back.

Flynn's lips quirk. "I've got money."

"Sorry," I say. "I'll pay next time. I know we're not dating." I punch the elevator button several times because I'm embarrassed.

I have money, too, now. I still work in the building—cleaning and nannying for Ravil, the bratva *pakhan*, but that is just to give me purpose. Adrian extorted five million dollars from Kat's father when he kidnapped her, so the three of us are now rich.

Flynn nudges me back against the elevator wall, his hands lightly resting on my waist. It's amazing how welcome his touch is. Normally even a brush from another person gives me the hives.

He lowers his head and captures my lips, stealing my breath. I feel the reverberation of the kiss between my legs—a slow pulsing that revs my nearly-dead sex drive back to life.

I drink Flynn in. He represents everything I want—the embodiment of carefree youth, of possibility, of living moment-to-moment. Sucking the juice out of life.

When I stand at the window in our apartment and look down at the world outside the building, I yearn to be someone like Flynn. But it seems so impossible. Like there's

39

an invisible barrier at the door to the building, and the moment I pass through it, I go mad.

When the elevator doors open on the ground floor, I'm breathless and horny.

But then things get hard. We're leaving the building. Going out into the world–something I hate.

There will be people out there. Strangers. Voices and bodies and the possibility of drowning in shadows again. I know that's not logical. I'm safe. I'm free. I haven't been fed drugs and chained to a bed for months now. And it will never happen again. Adrian has promised. My therapist assures me.

But my body still goes into fight or flight at the tiniest tweak of my senses.

I keep my lips closed and try to suck slow breaths in through my nose. I can do this. I'm with Flynn.

Everything is fine.

I can do this. I can do this. The sound of grinding gears grows louder around my head. My focus narrows and goes fuzzy.

Fuck. Am I breathing? I might pass out.

"Hey." I hear Flynn's voice, but it's from far away. Except he's standing right next to me. "Climb on my back."

I blink. Flynn turns and bends his knees, holding his arms out from his sides.

"What?" The grinding gears sound fades.

"Hop on."

I'm so confused. Did I miss something? Was the world spinning for longer than it seemed?

"Why?" My focus starts to return.

"So I can carry you," he says as if it makes perfect sense. As if I'm in bare feet, and we need to cross over crushed glass.

I'm able to draw in a deep breath through my nose. I use it to leap onto Flynn's back, wrapping my legs around his waist. He tucks his hands under my knees and starts to jog with me, whirling and tilting like a drunken sailor.

A surprised laugh tumbles from my lips. "What are you doing?"

"Taking you for a ride."

The shadows lift. The mechanical whirring stops completely. I close my eyes, savoring the moment. The icy air against my face. The immense gratitude in my heart for this kind-hearted man.

Just like that, I'm firmly back in my body. I can breathe. I'm not afraid. I'm actually…having fun. It seems impossible, and yet it's happening. To me.

"Do you want to go to the lake?" I ask. I've never been. I live in a building that overlooks Lake Michigan and have never even been the block it takes to walk to the shore. All this time, I've looked out our living room windows and watched the people down below. The joy of children running on the sand. The joggers along the walkway. The families nested under sun umbrellas and the joyful souls flying kites. I watch the boats float out on the water.

I've dreamed of what it would be like to come out here and join the living. But I haven't dared. But with Flynn, it seems possible. Almost anything seems possible with Flynn.

"You want to go to the lake?" he asks. "It will be cold. But I guess, you're from Russia, so you probably won't mind. We could get our coffees and take them with us to keep us warm."

"That sounds nice."

Flynn spins our bodies in a few more whirls and then careens through the doorway of a coffee shop. There, he lowers me to my feet. I look around. There are people in the shop. People I don't know. Strangers. But they're all talking amongst themselves. In their own worlds. No one even looks at us. I wait for the familiar sense of panic to rise, so I can stave it back down, so I can tell myself I'm fine because I'm here with Flynn. But it never comes. I truly am fine. Flynn is magic.

He leads me up to the counter and says, "What would you like?"

I am unafraid. Absolutely fearless. I look the barista right in her eye and say "I'll have a mocha."

"Make that two." Flynn pulls a ten dollar bill from his pocket.

I beam, marveling at how simple and easy that was. How I'm not even scared right now. We take our mochas outside where we walk toward the shore side by side. The drink is warm and sweet. When I slow to sip it, Flynn matches my pace.

That seems to be his gift.

"Where did you and Story learn to play guitar?" I ask.

"Our dad teaches guitar and plays in a local band–the Nighthawks. They do 80's rock covers."

"So you take after him."

"That's what they say." There's something hollow about the way Flynn says it. With anyone else, I wouldn't pry. Hell, with anyone else, I wouldn't attempt small talk. But we have a connection. He's seen me cry and didn't act like I was broken.

"Is it a bad thing?"

Again, I'm certain there's a ripple of discomfort in Flynn. A little flinch, perhaps. But he shakes his head. "No, he's cool."

"I would like to see his band, too."

This earns me a wide grin. "You would?"

Oh wow. Did I say that out loud? "Well–" I start to backpedal, panicking at committing myself to any outing, but Flynn says, "That would be fun. They don't play that often anymore, but I'll find out when their next gig is."

I draw in a breath, again bracing against the panic that doesn't come. All I sense is...excitement. A future date with Flynn. Getting to know him better.

But when we get to the lake, the crowd thickens. My steps falter, and I crowd closer to Flynn. He takes my mocha from my hand and turns around. "Hop on my back again."

I want to refuse. I want to go on like there's nothing wrong with me. Like I can make it through this. But he's offering me a branch, and I'm about to drown, so it take it. The mochas spill and slosh over his wrists when I jump on him. "Oh no!" I start to slide back down, embarrassed.

"No, no, no, no. We are fine." He hands one mocha back and uses his free hand to hold one of my knees. "Let's do this, Peaches."

I shriek and giggle when he takes off running again. I hold my coffee cup out to the side, so it won't spill on his head. He carries me to a park bench and holds me over the seat, releasing my leg. I stand on the bench and accept the hand he offers to jump down.

My stomach clenches when I see all the people, but Flynn sits and catches my waist. He tugs me forward, facing him, gently urging me onto his lap, straddling his waist.

It feels both natural and crazy at once.

"Look at me," he says, taking the mocha from my hand and setting it on the bench beside us. "It's just you and me out here," he says. "This is our world. No one else's."

I know what he's saying isn't true, and yet I cling to it as I lock onto his warm brown gaze.

He holds the eye contact, daring me to look away. "Kiss me."

I do. I lean forward and cover his lips with mine. He hasn't shaven today, so his face is scruffy. I like the contrast of rough stubble framing his soft, supple lips.

He grips my ass through my soft leggings, kneading it roughly, surprising me by working a finger between the seam of my ass cheeks.

For as much as I hate physical contact, as much as every nightmare is about intrusion, and my body not being under my own command, nothing about the way Flynn touches me is a trigger.

Not only does it not trigger me, but it stokes my fire. I squirm over his lap as my body comes to life, that pulsing between my legs growing more insistent. I grind down, seeking friction against my most sensitive parts.

When I feel the answering bulge in his jeans, I feel more triumphant than frightened. I was right in asking Flynn to be the guy who helps me get over my captivity. My doubts clear. I *do* want to have sex with him. I'm not afraid. With him, I could find sexual healing. I wish we could go back to the apartment right now, but Adrian is there.

I am so into the kiss I don't notice the people around me or the cold. Nothing takes my focus away from my own physical pleasure. The tangle of my tongue with Flynn's, the pressure of my clit over the seam of his jeans.

Nothing distracts me until I hear a woman's Russian-accented voice say with delighted interest, "Oh my God, is that Flynn? Looks like he met someone at the show again last night."

4

Flynn

I want to kill Sasha and Maxim for the interruption. They are another couple from the Kremlin—roommates of Story and Oleg. They often come to our gigs, but I didn't see them last night. Maxim is high up in the bratva—I'm guessing second-in-command. Sasha is an actress. They're dressed in jogging clothes and are breathing heavily, obviously out here for a run.

Nadia scrambles off my lap and onto her feet. I don't follow because I need a moment to shield my boner.

"Nadia!" Sasha gasps when she realizes the girl I was groping on my lap wasn't some random hookup from the show. "I didn't recognize you with your new hairstyle. It looks great!"

Maxim glares at me and growls, "Oh no" in a forbidding tone, like I just crashed into his car.

I normally like these two. Sasha is fun and personable, and Maxim is semi-approachable when she's on his arm. Right now, though, he looks like he wants to kick my ass. Story of my life with these guys lately.

"Flynn." He lifts a stern brow. "I know you're a player." He points at Nadia. "*Do not* play with this one."

"Okay." Nadia gives a nervous, breathy laugh.

"I mean it." He trains his finger at me now.

"Maxim," Sasha protests.

"No, no," Nadia rushes in. "I *asked* Flynn to have sex with me."

Aw, Christ.

"As friends," she clarifies. "We are friends with benefits."

"I can't see how they need to know that," I mutter.

"Okay," Sasha says, tugging on Maxim's arm as she backs up. "You heard her. It's Nadia's choice."

Maxim looks from me to Nadia and back again, still frowning. Apparently, he isn't finished. He pins me with a dangerous look. "You hurt this girl, and I will rip your spine out of your body."

"Provocative imagery." I stand, unfolding my long form from the bench, my boner now under control. "Not the first time my life has been threatened when it comes to Nadia." I meet his gaze without aggression but also without fear.

These guys want to protect Nadia, and I respect that. Something bad has happened to her; that's quite clear. But they have no idea what's going on between the two of us, and it really isn't any of their business. Also, Nadia gets to choose for herself.

"Yeah, every guy in the building will take turns eating your liver with a fork."

"Too much," Sasha chides, wrapping her arms around Maxim's waist and trying to pull him back.

"Enough," Nadia says with authority.

It must be a new tone for her because both Sasha and Maxim snap their gazes to her with surprise.

"No disrespect, but the only person I'm going to listen to about Nadia is Nadia." I say it firmly with a hint of challenge in my gaze.

I'm not stupid. I know I would lose a fight against this guy, but that doesn't mean I'd go down without swinging.

Maxim contemplates me for a moment. "You do you, Flynn," he says. "I'm just telling you what the consequences will be if she gets hurt."

"Noted."

"Okay, moving on!" Sasha tugs Maxim away, giving Nadia an enthusiastic wave and thumbs up as the two leave.

"I'm sorry," Nadia moans, turning back to me. A blush covers her peaches and cream complexion.

I shrug. "It's all good." I'm not going to get my feathers ruffled over people looking out for Nadia. I'm glad she has so many saviors.

Her phone rings, and she startles, like no one ever calls her. I make a mental note to change that. I'm already planning the late night calls from bed. The kind where you tell each other everything–all your deepest thoughts and feelings.

She scrambles to pull it out of her jacket pocket and answer. "Hi, Adrian."

I can't hear her brother's exact words, but his tone is loud and tense, like last night, when he couldn't find her outside of Rue's lounge.

"I'm at the lake with Flynn," she says.

There's a pause, and then I detect surprise in Adrian's answer. He speaks a little more, and then Nadia says, "okay" and hangs up.

When she looks at me she wears a mischievous smile. "They are leaving the apartment."

It takes me just a second to catch her implication. She wants to go back there. We can be unsupervised.

I take her hand. "Let's go."

Nadia walks beside me with a light step, darting glances my way. She's excited–she wants to have sex. I haven't had planned sex like this since I was in middle school. Yes, I started young.

I've had a lot of sex with a lot of different girls. They aren't conquests to me. I'm not trying to "hit that" or notch the bedpost. It's just something that happens naturally. I vibe with someone, I want to share pleasure. I don't get attached. I'm careful to ensure they don't, either.

My mom says it's in my DNA. She and my dad broke up and got back together nine times during our childhood before they finally called it quits for good, and it was always over dad cheating. With him, sex seems more like an addiction. Like he craves or requires the sex to prove something to himself. My gut tells me it's related to the band. They never made it big, but playing in the Nighthawks did bring him women, so he uses sex to make up for dashed dreams.

That might be why I never try too hard at anything. I sensed my dad's frustration and wanted no part of it. I play music because I love it, not because I'm trying to get to a destination. The fact that we've started gaining popularity since we did the Youtube collab with Skate 32 almost makes me uncomfortable. I don't want to get used to this success in case it evaporates and leaves me disappointed.

I'm not entirely sure what I'm walking into with Nadia. I try not to overthink it. I'm the kind of guy who goes with the flow–I play off others and improvise as necessary. I don't have an agenda here. I didn't come to get laid, but I'm also happy to be of service.

When we get back to the building, the front doors are

open. The big guard dog is sitting at the front desk. The guy who hates me.

"Hi Maykl." Nadia gives him a wave and shy smile as we come in, and his eyes nearly bug out of his head.

"Nadia," he says in surprise. "You were out."

I don't like the way her face colors, and she seems disconcerted. I wonder if her anxiety might be more pervasive than I'd realized. It sounds like she doesn't go out at all. Except that doesn't make sense because she's come to my shows a number of times. She definitely leaves the building.

"Yeah." She sounds breathless. "I went to the lake with Flynn. You know Flynn? From the Storytellers?"

The giant, heavily-tattooed Russian nods without giving me a smile.

"Hey." I lift my hand.

He doesn't return the gesture.

Whatever.

I follow Nadia to the elevator, and she pulls out her keycard to get us on.

"Heavy security in this building," I observe.

A shadow crosses her face. "It's good," she says. "We are safe here."

I hate that she hasn't felt safe. That security is something she clings to and needs. I want to remedy it for her, but I don't know how, other than to keep distracting her in the moments when she's afraid. Just like I distract my mom from her pain.

I kiss her again because it always seems to work, and she lightens up. When the elevator door opens, her laugh is breathy, and she breezes off.

"Come on." She looks over her shoulder with a smile as she jogs toward her apartment.

I follow her in, whistling when I see the view from the

floor-to-ceiling windows. "Damn, this place is fine." I look around as I take off my leather jacket and drape it over the back of the sofa. I've seen Story's place, which is just a bedroom connected to the top floor penthouse where a bunch of the head bratva live. It has every luxury, but I figured it was because the building's owner lives there. Now I'm thinking every apartment in the building must be pimped out. The apartment isn't huge, but it has a large, open living area with a kitchen to the left and the living room straight ahead. The kitchen features granite countertops and expensive cabinets. "The rent here must cost a fortune." I can't even guess how much–ten grand a month for a Chicago high rise with Lake Michigan views?

"We don't pay anything," Nadia says. "Ravil gave Adrian this place when he joined the bratva."

"Wow." I don't even want to think what that means Adrian must do for the guy. His soul has definitely been sold. "Ravil takes good care of his people."

"Yes." She drops her jacket and hat beside mine. "Want to see my room?"

I catch that hint of naughtiness in her again, and it makes me smile as I follow her into a large bedroom. It seems to have huge windows as well, but the shades are completely closed. The room is filled with fabric and a sewing machine stands on the desk.

"You sew?"

It suddenly makes sense–a lot of her clothing has that one-of-a-kind look–with special cuts or added fabric pieces. Like the leggings she's wearing today–she probably cut the slits in them herself.

"Yes. I studied fashion design in Russia, and I used to do alterations for wedding gowns."

I scan the bulletin board which has dozens of pictures

ripped from fashion magazines, along with hand-sketched items.

My eye's caught by a guy with a guitar. "Is that me?" I unpin the drawing to inspect it. Instead of my usual hipster casual clothing, the guy is wearing a slightly punk look–more like what Story sports to the shows. Skinny black jeans and a red sleeveless collared shirt with the collar turned up.

"Oh! Um, yes." She snatches the drawing and crumples it up.

"Hey," I protest.

"I want to style the band if you do another video," she blurts, tossing the drawing in the trash. "I have ideas."

"Yeah," I say.

She goes still, like she hadn't been expecting me to agree so easily. "Yes? I can?"

I shrug. "Sure. Yeah. I mean, I don't know how much we can pay you. We're only just starting to make a living from the shows."

"No, *nyet*. You don't pay me. I want to do it. You will let me?"

I make a scoffing sound. "Of course." I shrug. "I don't know when we're doing another video, though."

She blinks at me. "Would you wear them for a show?"

"Maybe? I don't know–our shows are pretty casual."

She gnaws on her lower lip, and I feel like an asshole.

"You know who always needs new costumes, though?"

"Who?"

"The burlesque dancers–Black Velvet Burlesque. They perform at Rue's Lounge on Friday nights–no, it's Thursdays now–it used to be Fridays. Have you ever been?"

"I don't know what this is."

"Burlesque? It's cool. I would say it's like a cross between performance art and stripping. Tastefully bawdy.

Sometimes funny. Always entertaining." When Nadia stares at me blankly, I say, "You have to see for yourself. I'll take you this week, okay?"

She nods, eagerly. "Yes, I would like that."

Huh. That feels like a date. Not that getting coffee this morning and walking to the lake didn't. I'm a guy who literally never dates. It's one of the lines in the sand I won't cross. I don't lead girls on, which means sex is for sex only. There's no dating as foreplay or any other make-believe relationship shit.

I'm not cut out for relationships, so I don't give women the impression that I'd ever stick around.

But Nadia and I are friends. Friends with benefits.

I'd get coffee or see a show with Ty or Lake. So there's nothing wrong with taking Nadia to see a burlesque show.

Still, I get those warning bells–the same ones I got when I agreed to this whole friends-with-benefits plan. Like there's a catch somewhere that I'm not seeing. Something's going to stick me, and I'll realize I fucked up.

For the moment, though, I can't see it. All I see is beautiful Nadia, taking off her boots, wanting my help in finding her pleasure.

And I intend to make sure she finds it.

I toe off my Converse high tops and open the shades a crack to let in the light.

"You don't want it dark?" Nadia's hands tangle in front of her waist, making me reach for them.

"I want to see you, but do you want it dark?"

"No," she says quickly. "No. I hate the dark. I–"

Seeing she's going someplace unpleasant, I pull her against my body and kiss her again. I could kiss this girl all day and all night.

With some women, I skip the kissing completely or pass through it quickly–and just get straight to the main event.

But with Nadia, it still feels like there's so much left to discover.

Like I'm that middle-schooler again, just learning what it means to kiss. Marveling at the softness of her lips, the responsiveness. Drinking in her mocha taste, stunned by the honor of having her body up against mine.

She returns the kisses, standing on her tiptoes, getting more animated. She starts making little sounds–like she's excited or impatient. I pull her sweater off over her head and toss it to the floor. Her bra is the cutest thing I've ever seen–pale peach cups covered with see-through black lace and a little satin bow at the base between her breasts.

"Oh my God, what is this, Peaches? You're so damn pretty." I mold my hands around the bra cups and squeeze, and she gives a husky laugh. "So…" I kiss from her jaw down the side of her neck. "Damn…" I slip my finger under her bra strap and pull it down her arm to kiss across her collarbone to her shoulder. "Pretty." I take a big bite of the meat of her shoulder–firm enough to make her gasp, gentle enough not to leave a mark.

I work open the clasp at the back of her bra and slide the other strap off her shoulder, so it drops to the floor. Her breasts are pale and peach-tipped. She gets nervous when I look, so I turn her to face out, toward the window that faces the lake. I cup both her breasts in my hands and squeeze, working her nipples into firm points between my thumbs and forefingers as I kiss along the side of her neck and nip her ear.

"Tell me what you want, Peaches."

She nods. "I want to do this."

Oh. Okay, I didn't know doing it or not was still in question. Good to know.

"How do you want it, Nadia?"

She shakes her head. "I…I don't know."

"Okay," I say. "You don't have to know." I stroke my palm up the flat plane of her belly, then back down, angling my hand into her leggings. I start over her panties, cupping her mons. The fabric of her panties is both smooth and rough. Satin and lace.

"Aw, Peaches. Are these matching?" I shove her leggings down her hips to get a look.

Damn.

"So sexy." I drop to a squat to pull her leggings and socks off her feet, leaving her in nothing but her panties. Then I trail my tongue up the inside of her leg, starting at her ankle and making my way with flicks and nips and brief sucking all the way to the apex of her thighs.

"You want my mouth here, pretty girl?"

She works to swallow. "Um…"

I wait because she seems unsure.

"I don't know."

I open my mouth and nip her pussy through her panties.

"No," she says quickly, and I instantly back off. "Um, I just want… to, um, you know." She flaps her hand and says something in Russian.

"Talk to me, Peaches."

She darts to the bed and climbs on it. "Let's… you know…"

"We might need to work on your dirty talk," I tease, following her to the bed. I peel my sweater and t-shirt off over my head and toss them to the floor with Nadia's clothes.

My dick is harder than a rock because Nadia is a wet dream in just her panties, but I leave my jeans on for the moment to remind myself this isn't for me. It's for her.

I would love to get her off with just my mouth or my

fingers. Give her some pleasure without feeling the need to reciprocate.

"I don't know dirty talk in English–"

I stop her with a kiss. "Kidding." I kiss her again. "I was just teasing. You're perfect, Peaches."

She wraps her arms around me and pulls me down on top of her for more kissing. I press my thigh between her legs to give her some friction as I sweep my tongue between her lips.

She kisses me back–passionately. Breathlessly.

And then too breathlessly.

There's a wild, mad scramble of limbs and nails and flying hair as a gasping Nadia fights her way out from beneath me.

"Nadia. Hang on. Are you okay?"

She struggles to breathe, her face turning red.

"Nadia, babe. Come here, let me help."

It's too late, though. She's totally freaked. She scrambles off the bed and runs out of the room.

Nadia

Can't. Breathe.

Blyad'. Blyad.' Blyad'.

Metal machinery parts clash and bang between my ears. Chain links clack.

I run for the bathroom, terror seizing all of my body. I'm shaking all over, freezing cold, and can't draw a breath for the life of me.

I knew it was Flynn, I wanted to be with Flynn, but then suddenly something transported me back to the sofa factory, and it was the cigar man on top of me, smothering me. Covering my mouth, so I couldn't breathe.

Bozhe moi, I'm so embarrassed. And heartbreakingly disappointed. And I still can't breathe. I struggle to get control of my body, but it won't cooperate.

"Nadia!"

Gah. Flynn's chasing me in here.

I try to shut the door on him, but he throws his arm between the door and the frame, keeping it from closing. I abandon my effort to shut him out and return to the more pressing concern—breathing. Trying to turn down the deafening clash of metal.

But I don't want Flynn to see me this way.

Dammit, I wanted to have my fantasy where Flynn and I made love and the violent non-consensual acts in my past would just fade away.

"Please," I gasp. "*Pozhaluysta*...please." I grip the bathroom countertop and hang my head, wheezing for breath. Stars dance before my eyes. The room starts to spin.

I hear the front door open and close, but it doesn't register.

Not until I hear the crack of a fist on flesh and see Flynn's body slam against the bathroom wall.

"Stop it!" I scream in Russian, throwing myself between my very pissed-off brother and an offended Flynn.

I understand why Adrian attacked. It must look bad with me in nothing but my panties begging Flynn to leave me alone, but for God's sake!

"Stop," I repeat in Russian, bursting into tears. I'm thankful for the sobs because at least they move my breath.

I realize now I was struggling to inhale the whole time, but I couldn't because I hadn't let my breath out. My lungs were already full of old air.

My body didn't even know how to breathe. That's how disconnected I am from it. It's no wonder after what happened to me. I had to leave my body just to keep my sanity those months I was chained in the basement of the sofa factory, pimped out as a sex slave in a country where I didn't speak a word of the language.

I should turn to face Flynn. To apologize, but I'm too embarrassed. Too terribly, horribly humiliated.

I invited him into this. This crazy shit-show. I asked him to have sex with me as a favor, then I freaked out, and then my brother punched his face in.

"I'm going to kill him." Adrian is still full of fury.

"*Hold* on." Kat wraps her arms around him from behind, trying to hold him back. As if she's any match for my brother.

Flynn gets back on his feet. "Dude, what the fuck?"

Adrian tries to lunge around me, but I block him. "I told you I would kill you if you touched her."

Flynn is less worried about Adrian than he is about me. He yanks a towel down from the rack and drapes it over my shoulders. "Nadia." He tries to turn me, but I can't look at him. I jerk away, which only further activates Adrian.

"*Nyet.* Don't fucking talk to her," Adrian snarls.

"Get out!" I sob. "All of you!"

"Adrian, you're making it worse. You're *not helping*," Kat says.

"You want me out, Nadia?" Flynn asks in a low voice. He has that talent for de-escalating things. Adrian gets louder, but Flynn gets softer. It makes the metal clanging quiet because I have to strain to hear him.

"Yes," I choke. "Please." I *hate* that he's seeing me like this.

It's so damn embarrassing.

"Come on." Kat tugs Adrian's arm. "That means us, too. Let Flynn leave."

I step into the shower not because I plan to use it, but to hide from all of them. I sink to my ass on the tile floor, plug my ears, and rock, trying to quiet the screech and scream of mechanical gears turning in my head.

"Nadia." Flynn gets even softer. He crouches outside the shower, giving me space, and picks up one of my hands. I expect him to ask if I'm okay, or tell me that it's okay, or do something that will require me to speak, but he doesn't say anything. He just squeezes my fingers and waits a moment then releases them and gets up and leaves.

The moment he walks away, I bite my hand on a sob.

5

Flynn

Kat pulls Adrian out of the bathroom and into the living room, where he regards me with a glower when I walk out.

"Get out," he growls and tosses my shirt, sweater and jacket at me.

I hesitate because I don't want to leave Nadia like this. I want to be with her through it. To sit beside her and hold her hand and distract her with something benign that helps her shift.

But she said she wanted me out, and I do suspect Adrian would kick my ass if I tried to stay.

Fuck, he throws a mean punch. I don't give him the satisfaction of seeing me rub my jaw although it's starting to throb.

"You have no idea what you're dealing with here. She can't do this with you. Now get out."

I hesitate a moment longer then leave the apartment. I step into the elevator and hit the button for the underground parking lot.

I honestly don't care about getting punched.

I'm in trauma over Nadia's trauma. I want to fix it for her. Fix everything.

Dammit, now I'm one hundred times more invested in making sure she gets everything she wants out of our non-relationship.

She needs sexual healing? I'm her man.

She needs a friend? I will be with her through thick and thin.

Hell, if she needed a *boy*friend, I'd be that for her, too.

I don't take the time to examine that thought because it's irrelevant. She doesn't want a boyfriend. She's just trying to get through her days.

The elevator doors open, and I step into the parking garage. Something about Nadia's breakdown makes me need to call my mom. I pull my phone out and dial her number as I walk to the van.

How many times have I been with her in moments like that? Dozens. Maybe more. At age sixteen, I was the guy who drove her to the psychiatric treatment center to check herself in because Story had the flu. I visited her there. Sat with her when she got out.

The episodes were scary when I was little, but I learned to lean into them. To show up for her. Hold her hand. Distract her. Lay my head on her shoulder.

"Flynn! How's my favorite son?" she answers. I'm her only son, so it's a little joke of hers.

"Hi, Mom. You sound good." I open the door to the van and climb behind the wheel but don't start it up.

"I am good. My friend Dan spent the night last night."

She means boyfriend. My mom doesn't really know how to do casual sex like my dad and me. She gets attached and then broken-hearted. It's hard to watch.

Thank fuck neither Story nor Dahlia–my two sisters–took after her. Story used to be more like me, but now they both are in serious relationships.

"That's great, Mom. Is he still there?"

"Yes. I'm making pancakes. Want to come over?"

"Eh, no. I don't want to interrupt. Have fun with Dan."

"Hang on. What's going on with you, sweetheart?"

"I just called to hear your voice."

"Aw, I love you, Flynn. But you can't fool me–I know when something's on your mind."

I grunt my agreement.

"What is it? What happened?"

"There's a girl…"

"*Oh.*"

I resent the surprise in my mom's voice, even though it's fully warranted.

"We're just friends," I clarified. "Nevermind."

"*Hang on* a second." She pulls out the mom voice that makes me straighten up and pay attention even though I'm twenty-two years old. "Tell me about her."

"She's Russian, like Oleg. She lives in Story's building and comes to our shows. I really like her."

"Go on."

"Well, something bad has happened to her–like a sexual assault kind of thing. She had a panic attack when we were, ah…"

"*Oh.*" My mom correctly interprets my hesitation. "Flynn, sweetheart, I've told you before. You don't have to have sex with every girl you like. Some can just stay friends."

I grunt. Not what I wanted her to say.

"You are such a nice guy. You like everyone you meet.

61

You're friendly with everyone. Sex isn't the only way to show that."

"Gee, thanks, Mom."

I definitely shouldn't have brought this up.

"No, listen to me. It sounds like this girl is already struggling emotionally. She doesn't need you to screw with her head and her heart. Maybe don't try to jump in the sack with this one, okay?"

Something pierces my chest at that and opens up a wound I didn't even know I had.

Why is everyone so sure I'm going to hurt Nadia?

I don't hurt women on a regular basis. I really don't. I'm honest. I communicate. I make my intentions clear.

And my intentions are usually…that nothing will come of us. That's truly the way I live my life. I don't try too hard because big dreams equal big disappointment. I learned that rule from my dad.

I don't try at relationships. I don't try at a career. I don't try with the band.

And I believe it's precisely that flow state that's created our current success. I mean, we couldn't have manufactured what happened with getting paired with Skate 32. It was a lucky break when Chelle and Nikolai brought the Youtube skate stars to see our show, and they wanted to collaborate with a couple videos for their fans.

So maybe that's the answer. I'm trying too hard here. I can't fix things for Nadia, and any time I try to succeed at something, it just gets difficult. "Yep, you're right," I tell my mom.

"What else is going on with you?" she asks.

"Nah, that's it. Go have your pancakes. Love you, Mom."

"I love you, too, sweetheart. Come by and see me soon."

"Yep. I will. Bye, Mom."

I start the van and drive home to my apartment. I lived with Ty and Lake until Story moved in with Oleg, and then I took over her apartment. I walk in and toss my keys on the table by the door.

It's weird living alone. I sort of hate it because I'm a social guy. I grew up with two sisters and a very dramatic and unstable mom and a dad who brought musicians in and out of the house at all hours. I thrive in chaos.

I also party too much, so my apartment is more of a place to crash than a home.

The place is a disaster—pizza boxes litter the coffee table. Empty beer bottles are all over the place. There are three roaches in the ashtray.

After being at Nadia's place, I see it through new eyes.

Or maybe I'm wondering how she would view it, if she came over. I start picking up the beer bottles and throwing them into the recycling box.

I don't know why I'm thinking about Nadia coming over. She won't.

She shouldn't.

My mom was right—whether my intentions were pure or not, having sex with Nadia was a mistake. My first instinct had been right. Keep her in the friend zone. Especially because she's a girl I care about more than most.

Nadia

I ruined everything.

I am so humiliated.

It took an eternity—at least forty-five minutes—before the screeching gears, hyperventilation and tears stopped. Then I just curled up on the bed, unable to move.

Kat makes chamomile tea and brings it to my room with a soft knock on the door. When I ignore her, she comes in and sets it on the dresser.

"Are you okay?" she asks softly.

"No." I huddle on the bed, looking through the open window shades at the blue water beyond. The Lake Michigan vista seems so expansive. So inviting.

I often keep these shades closed because the world feels too big when they're open. But Flynn opened them today, which makes me loath to close them again. He showed me possibilities beyond this bedroom. We even walked to the lake!

"May I give you a hug?"

I don't really want one, but I also don't want to refuse my brother's new girlfriend. She's only been here a few weeks, but she's already family. She's Adrian's whole world, and she loved me right from the start. She doesn't judge where I am. She wants to help. I know some of that comes from guilt because her dad ran the sex trafficking ring that I was enslaved in. But most of it is just who she is.

I roll over to face Kat and sit up when she comes to sit on the bed to embrace me.

"What happened?"

"Nothing." I start to cry again. "I don't know. I asked him to have sex with me—just as friends—and he agreed. But he was on top, and it triggered me. I freaked out, and then Adrian punched him. So now I'm sure he never wants to see me again." I cover my face with my hands. "I am totally humiliated."

"I don't think that's true," Kat says. "Flynn seemed really concerned about you."

I groan.

"Adrian shouldn't have attacked him. Maybe I can get him to apologize."

"No," I protest. "Adrian needs to butt out of this. It's none of his business."

"I know, you're right," Kat says. "I told him that. He's just worried about you and trying to protect you."

"Has he ever considered that his worry doesn't help me? I think it makes things worse." My vision blurs with fresh tears. As I speak the words I realize how true they are. It's Flynn's assumption that I am fine, that I can go outside, that I can walk to the lake, that makes me believe it's possible. When Adrian assumes I can't do anything, I believe him.

"I'm sorry." Adrian stands in the doorway, a tattooed forearm propped against the frame, his muscles bulging beneath his Henley.

He wasn't always like this—so dangerous and angry. I did this to him.

We've always looked out for each other. Our mother died of cancer when we were young, and our father drowned his grief in alcohol. We became close because we were all we had to rely on.

Adrian worked hard to get a degree in engineering and had a job doing maintenance and repair on ships. He was always tough and resourceful, but my kidnapping turned him into a killer. He's done things I don't want to know about. He joined the bratva to have access to the resources necessary to find me. And in the process, he became a much darker, more deadly version of himself.

I suck in a hiccuping breath. "I don't want to be like this anymore."

Pain etches in the lines around Adrian's eyes. I know he wants to fix it, but his overprotectiveness isn't helping.

"You need to let me do this in my own way."

His brow wrinkles. "Because you're doing such a good job of it on your own?"

"Adrian," Kat admonishes.

"Sorry," he says. "But seriously Nadia, is it working?"

Maybe he's right. My way was a total disaster. But that doesn't make his way right, either.

"Adrian, please go. I just want to be alone," I say.

He nods and leaves. Kat hesitates.

My phone buzzes with an incoming text. I almost never receive texts, so I snatch it up to look at the screen, then show it to Kat. "It's him." All of the slowness in my world speeds up. I open the text.

"He says *hey*. What does that mean?" I understand the English word *hey*, but reading context into a text message might be beyond my language level.

"He's reaching out." Kat gives me a smile of encouragement. "It's just an opening. Sort of an invitation for you to respond–but without pressure."

That sounds exactly like Flynn. As I hold the phone in both hands, some of the leaden weight in my body melts away. Kat slips off the bed and leaves the room as I type the word *hey* in response.

Can I call? he texts.

Heart thudding, I hit the call button next to his name. He answers with the same word he texted, "Hey."

"Hey." Warmth floods my chest even though it's one word. Hearing his voice changes my state faster than seems possible.

"I'm really sorry about Adrian," I say. "Are you okay?"

"Yeah. It's cool. Are you okay?" There is so much gentle kindness in the question that I have to fight back tears again. But they feel so different this time. They're not filled with bitterness and defeat. It's more the watering eyes that comes from knowing that someone cares about me.

"I'm okay," I choke. "I'm sorry, I–"

"Don't be sorry," he cuts in. "There's nothing to be sorry for. You told me something bad happened to you."

He says nothing more as if leaving space for me to fill in without the pressure of a question. He's not asking, but he's available if I want to talk.

"Yes. Something bad happened to me," I say. "Something really bad."

"Yeah." That's all he says. Again there's an openness. So much space here in the room, so much invitation between us. I'm not suffocating.

I don't tell this story, ever. I've told pieces to Adrian, but he already knew the meat of it. I never had to start from the beginning.

What was the beginning? Oh. I remember.

"You know that wedding dress shop I told you I worked in?"

"Yeah."

"I worked late sometimes. We had rush orders, and wedding dresses can't be late, you know? So I was there alone until midnight one night." I swallow, not wanting to go on. "I locked up. I walked toward my car, and someone grabbed me in the parking lot."

I hear Flynn suck in a breath, but he says nothing.

"I fought. I know what they say–fight for your life because once they get you in a vehicle, no one will ever see you again." Images flash in front of my eyes. The three men who closed in on me. The light they used to blind me. "I slipped on ice trying to get away. When I fell, I banged my knee on the pavement." It's funny, I'd forgotten about my knee until now. *Gospodi*, it swelled up like a balloon. So did my face where they hit me until I blacked out.

I push back the torment. There were so many torments, but that one seems the freshest. The very first violence inflicted on me.

67

I clear my throat. "I, uh, passed out. And when I woke, I was chained to a bed." My voice sounds like it's coming from far away. I must be leaving my body just to tell this story.

A strangled sound comes through the phone, and Flynn's breath rasps in, but he seems to hold back whatever he was going to say.

"There were other women. I don't know how many." Fourteen of us survived. That's how many were left when Adrian freed us. They hit us and drugged us and sold our bodies many, many times.

"No." Flynn's voice is a broken whisper. I don't want to give him this pain. It's too much to give anyone. Too horrible to recount.

"I'm sorry. You shouldn't have to hear this. It's…not a good topic."

Flynn says nothing, and I assume he agrees—that it was too much to lay on him. But then he says, "Tell me the rest."

"The rest." I draw in a sharp breath and let it out slowly. "They put us in a shipping container on a boat."

The crew raped us every night, all night, as payment for our passage. I wanted to die. My days and nights were one long nightmare. Because they kept us drugged, I was confused and hazy and sick all the time.

"Fuck."

"Somehow we ended up here in Chicago, in the basement of a sofa factory."

"What?" Flynn sounds shocked.

"Yeah. Chained to cots again. With choke collars and leashes. Customers came in and used us there." One customer came for me every night. The same horrible man. The one with the cigars.

Gospodi. I can't tell him. The image of the fat man's

sneer flits before my eyes, and I hear the clang of metal in my ears.

To keep the panic at bay, I keep talking. "We never left. Never saw daylight. Didn't know where we were, other than guessing America because the customers spoke English."

Flynn says nothing. He just leaves a big space of silence for me to go on if I choose.

Faintly, in the distance, I still hear the clink of metal. The tightness in my chest that precedes a panic attack.

I push on, wanting to get to the end of the story without freaking out. Keep it short and get through the worst of it. "I lost all hope. I thought we'd never get free. Me and the others. But Adrian found us."

"Thank fuck."

"*Da.* He freed us all and burned the place down."

When Flynn still leaves the space open, I give him the last shocking tidbit. "Kat's father was the leader of the sex traffickers, and Adrian kidnapped her as bait, so he could kill her dad."

"Jesus," Flynn mutters.

"But he fell in love and brought her home instead."

I hear Flynn's soft breath on the other side. He's here with me. Listening.

"Her dad is awaiting trial in Europe, but Adrian got him to pay five million dollars for her before he went to jail, and the three of us split the money."

"Wow."

The story sounds unbelievable, even though I lived through it. I know it's all true.

"So...That's why I am sort of broken."

"You're not broken," he says immediately as if it's fact. "You're definitely not broken. Far from it. Nadia, you're brave and bright and full of life. You're just coming out of your chrysalis. I already see your wings."

"What is *chrysalis*? I don't know this word."

"The cocoon a butterfly comes from."

I smile against the phone. "Thank you. I like that. You make me forget what I am. Or maybe you make me remember who I used to be. Except we can never go back, can we? So it's not who I used to be, but who I will be."

I'm rambling, but Flynn seems there for it.

"See? You're a chrysalis about to become a butterfly." I hear the smile in Flynn's voice.

"Can we try again?"

When Flynn hesitates, my heart jumps into my throat and clogs my breath. I bunch the blankets in my fist and pull them up to my chin.

I did ruin things. Why would he want to try again with me? I made a total fool out of myself and got him punched in the face for his efforts.

"Everyone thinks I'm going to hurt you," Flynn says after a few beats.

I still can't breathe. I force out a little shaky exhale, remembering how it works. "What do you think?"

"I want to do this with you."

My heart resumes its beating.

"And I would never hurt you. At least not purposely."

"But?" I ask because I still hear the hesitation in his voice.

"But I don't do relationships."

I try to ignore the heat rushing to my face, the tears that want to fall again.

Is he saying no? Is this our breakup? Of course, we can't have a breakup because we never were an item to begin with. I latch on to that fact and offer it back to him.

"I'm not asking for a boyfriend. I told you that. I'm in no shape for a relationship, anyway."

"Yeah, same," Flynn says.

"Why don't you have relationships?" I ask.

"It's just too much pressure, and I can barely be responsible for my own life."

I sense a cop-out there, and I want to call him on it, but not while we're dancing around the topic of us.

"Have you ever had a girlfriend?" It's none of my business, but I just shared my ugliest secret with him, so it seems only fair to ask him to share something back.

"I had a girlfriend in middle school," he says. "She was my first."

"First girlfriend?"

He gives a rough laugh. "Yes, but I meant the first girl I had sex with."

"And what happened?"

"It got really intense." Flynn's voice is low and gravelly like this secret is just for me. "She was super possessive and freaked out on me if I didn't call her every day after school or if I did anything with anyone else. Things got pretty bad before I finally broke it off."

"I guess you're the kind of guy a girl wants to hang on to," I say. I certainly understand the urge. To be in Flynn's field of attention is to bask in the sunlight. He's definitely a guy worth keeping.

But I don't ever want to be that clingy girl to Flynn. I won't be.

And then I wonder what it would take for Flynn to feel that way about a girl. What kind of woman would make him get possessive the way Adrian is possessive of Kat? What female could make Flynn want to be with her all hours of the day? To want to know where she is and what she's doing at all times. To want to be her everything.

"How old were you when you had this girlfriend?" I don't know what *middle school* means in America.

"Fourteen."

"Fourteen? Oh God," I laugh. "I was stupid with boys at fourteen, too. I'm not sure you should completely write off relationships based on that experience."

He gives a low chuckle. "Maybe not, but I'm not looking for anything intense."

Again, I want to call bullshit. He isn't afraid of intensity. He's unflinching in the face of my panic attacks. In the face of getting punched in the face for trying to calm me down when I freaked out after attempting sex. He's the opposite of afraid. I want to root out the real reason behind his reluctance to take on a girlfriend, but I shouldn't care. I don't want that, anyway.

I finally work up enough courage to bring up the topic of sex with me again. "So, was that a no? I don't blame you for not wanting to try again with me."

"Nah, we're definitely having sex. I'm totally down."

My heart skips a beat. "Yes?"

"Yes."

"When?"

"We're going to the burlesque show Thursday, right?" he reminds me.

A fluttering in my chest starts up. We have a date. One I wasn't sure was even happening. "Yes."

"The Storytellers have our rehearsal at the Kremlin on Thursday this week," he tells me.

My heart flutters just knowing he'll be in the building in a few days. Thursdays have long been the highlight of my week for those chance—or sometimes orchestrated to seem like chance—meetings with Flynn in the hallway before or after.

"We could hang out after rehearsal and then go to the show."

"Yes," I say as if he's asking me to marry him. I don't know how us watching the burlesque dancers will turn into sex, but it doesn't matter.

I'll be with Flynn.

There have been many days these past months when I could barely get myself out of bed because of depression and anxiety, but when I'm with Flynn, I feel like I'm alive again.

"Great. I'll see you Thursday."

Thursday. Four long days away.

"Yes, okay. See you Thursday."

I end the call and press the phone to my chest. I have a date.

Non-date. Whatever.

I'm going to see Flynn again, and maybe this time, I won't freak out.

CHAPTER 6

Flynn

I stick around in the studio after rehearsal Thursday, trying out some new riffs on the guitar. What we're doing with the band doesn't feel like enough anymore. What I'm doing with my life doesn't feel like enough, either.

Knowing Nadia's walking around trying to rebuild her life after having so much taken from her suddenly makes my lackadaisical approach to living feel empty.

I carried the weight of Nadia's pain all week. It's not a burden. I know I chose to pick it up. But, fuck, if I could help it! My eyes burned, and I wanted to cry like a fucking baby when she told me.

And then when she asked if we could try again, I was even more conflicted. On one hand, it seemed like even my mom was right. Nadia had way too much going on emotionally to forge any kind of relationship with someone right now, particularly not a sexual one.

But, of course, like the first time she asked, I was also incapable of denying her anything at all.

She wants sex from me? She can have it. As much as

she needs for as long as she needs. I will make it my life's mission to ensure she gets exactly the kind of sex she needs to recover from her trauma.

But I can't pretend that knowing her story didn't change me. It did.

"You staying?" Lake asks me when I don't pack up.

"Yeah. Oh, hang on, Story. I need you to use your keycard in the elevator, so I can pick Nadia up." I unplug my guitar and shove it in its case.

"You're picking Nadia up?"

Damn. Ty, Lake, Story, and Oleg all stare at me now, wanting the full scoop.

I shrug, forcing myself to look casual, which is usually my only way of being. "Yeah, she wants to see the burlesque show at Rue's."

"She does?" Story's brow wrinkles and I suddenly realize that she might know Nadia's story. Damn her for not telling me although I guess it's not her story to tell. No pun intended.

"Yeah. She might make their costumes. And she wants to style us if we do another video."

"What?" Lake asks. "What does that mean?"

"She's a fashion designer. That's what she did in Russia. She has ideas for the band." I don't know why, but it seems desperately important that I help define Nadia as something other than a victim to everyone around her.

"That's cool," Ty says.

"Wow, I didn't know that," Story says, getting in the elevator with Oleg. I follow them on. Ty and Lake wait for one going down.

When the doors shut, Oleg inserts his key card and presses the button for Nadia's floor. When the elevator starts, Oleg signs something to me.

I look to Story for interpretation, but she makes an

impatient sound. "You won't learn if you don't try, Flynn," she says. Oleg, her giant bratva fiance, had his tongue cut out by his old boss. Story has insisted that we all–Oleg included–learn American Sign Language, so we can communicate with him.

I'm not around him enough to have picked much up yet.

"Okay, try it again," I say, watching intently.

The elevator stops on Nadia's floor. Oleg blocks my path and repeats the sign.

The only thing I recognize is the sign for *sorry*.

"He says, sorry, but he has to accompany you until he knows you're authorized to be there since it was his keycard."

"Huh," I mutter. The three of us walk down the hall together. "Let me ask you this, Oleg. If Adrian tries to beat my ass for taking Nadia out again, whose side are you on?"

Oleg's face remains impassive, which is normal for him. I know it drives Story crazy because it's part of his non-communicative thing. When he catches Story looking at him expectantly, he signs something.

"He says he won't let Adrian hurt you."

"Okay, I wasn't asking for a bodyguard. I was just wondering if I had to worry about two of you now."

"Oleg wouldn't hurt you," Story says immediately.

I'm sure she believes that. I know Oleg would never hurt her, and that sentiment may extend to me as her brother, but I also suspect bratva loyalties run deep.

I knock on Nadia's door, and Adrian answers it with a glower. "I brought Oleg to kick your ass if you punch me again," I say.

Adrian's gaze jerks to Oleg's.

"Just kidding. He's here because I'm not allowed to roam free in the Kremlin."

Adrian lifts his chin at Oleg, which I interpret to mean that he's taking over the watch now. It's funny how just because Oleg doesn't speak, people don't speak much to him, either. I think it drives Story crazy. That's why she pushes us all to learn sign language.

"Did you punch Flynn?" Story asks, sounding shocked. She searches my face, her gaze locating the yellowing bruise on my jaw.

"Uh uh," I cut off her questioning. "I don't need you to stick up for me." I lean over and kiss the top of her head because my big sister is much shorter than I am. "You guys can go now–*bye*," I say pointedly.

Adrian steps into the hallway and shuts the door like I'm not allowed in their apartment.

Aw, fuck. Is he going to try to keep me from seeing her altogether?

"I'm not going to apologize for hitting you," he growls, which actually relaxes me. It means he at least knows he *should* apologize.

"Nah, you do you, bro. I understand. Nadia told me what happened."

This changes him. I suddenly see the full weight of the horrors she endured in the lines of his face, the weight on his beefy shoulders. Just like I'd carried the weight of her pain all week–willingly. This guy's been living with it 24/7 for so much longer than I have. Who can blame him for lashing out and trying to erase any additional stressors that come her way?

"So you see why this can't happen–especially not with you." He points back and forth between me and the door.

I take exception to the *especially not with you* part.

"She's not ready. She doesn't leave apartment." Adrian's accent has grown thick.

78

"She does. She did." I spread my hands. "She leaves it with me."

Adrian opens his mouth like he's going to argue, but I plow on.

"Listen, I know you're holding her up–you've been holding her together ever since you rescued her. But at some point, you have to see that you're also holding something in place."

Adrian jerks back like I punched him. "What thing?"

"Who you think she is right now. Nadia wants to change. She can't do it if you're keeping the broken version of her in place."

Adrian's brows slam down, and his upper lip curls, but just then Nadia throws open the door and demands something in Russian. "Hi." She turns that moonbeam smile on me, and my insides bunch up in my chest. She looks breathless and happy to see me. I want to kiss her senseless.

"Hi. You look great." She has on knee-high boots with a pair of black jeans and a sweater that criss-crosses at her throat, leaving both shoulders bare. Her new shag bob with the copper highlights perfectly frames her face. She looks *hot.*

Adrian grumbles something in Russian and stalks back inside. I take it as his acceptance of our date.

"I'm sorry about Adrian, he didn't threaten you again, did he?"

I shake my head. "No. It's cool."

"Um." She rubs her lips together. She's wearing lip gloss, and I already want to know how it tastes. "I'll just grab my jacket."

"Cool."

"Cool," she echoes, a secret smile on her face as she slips back inside. Then she immediately throws the door open, grabs my hand, and pulls me inside. "You don't have to wait in the hallway. You're welcome in our home."

"Hey, Flynn," Kat calls out from the kitchen. Her accent is an interesting mix of British-English and Slavic. Like she learned English in the UK not here. She's sitting on the kitchen counter, licking a spoon with peanut butter. She wears her long, dark hair in pigtails and has on white thigh-high socks and a plaid schoolgirl skirt. Adrian hovers near her, indulgent, but protective.

Now that I know their origin story, my interest is piqued.

"Don't worry about curfew." She beams a wide, saucy grin. "We trust you completely."

It's funny because we all know the opposite is true—at least from Adrian's point of view—so I chuckle, immediately liking Kat. "Yeah, I really got that," I say drily.

"I'm ready." Nadia has put on a bright red woolen jacket, belted at the waist, and she tugs me toward the door.

Nadia calls out something in Russian, and I give Adrian and Kat a wave as we leave. I catch her hand in mine on the way to the elevator. I don't see any of the nervousness in her that I saw the last time we left the apartment. Her hand isn't clammy. She's not relaxed, but her manner is more excited than scared.

As if reading my mind, when we get in the elevator, she says, "I think I'm going to be fine. I feel fine!"

"You're totally fine." I bring the back of her hand to my lips and kiss it, inhaling her butterscotch scent. I don't know what I'm doing. We're supposed to be friends. Friends who have sex.

Do friends with benefits hold hands and exchange little gestures of intimacy? I sort of doubt it, but I don't want to stop. It feels too right to hold Nadia's hand in mine. To receive the pleasure of her company. To have the honor of my lips on her skin.

"If not, you already know I'm cool chilling in the back of the van for as long as you need."

She laughs, which was my intention. "I won't need to." She seems confident, and I take in the new Nadia. I'm not sure what changed her, but she definitely seems different. Much happier.

There's a lifeforce fizzing and bubbling in her that I didn't see so much before.

I take her to the parking garage, and we ride to Rue's in the band's van. It belongs to both Story and me because it was a hand-me-down from our dad when we formed the band because it's big enough to haul sound equipment and instruments. I usually drive it, but I also have a motorcycle, and Story has a small Smart Car.

"What kind of music do you like?" I ask, changing the dial on the radio.

"I like your music," she says.

"Aw, you *are* a peach, aren't you?" I keep fiddling with the dial until I hit a pop station where I leave it. "What did you listen to in Russia?"

"Rock." She looks over at me. "Did you always want to have a band?"

I shrug. "It just seemed like something I would naturally do because of my dad. It was less something I wanted and more just inevitable. Ty and Lake and I all went to high school together and started the band. We thought a female lead singer would be a good draw, so we talked Story into fronting for us."

"She's good," Nadia agrees. "But I would like to see you on lead vocals."

"Nah." I immediately dodge that expectation like I

dodge relationships. I wouldn't want to be pinned down or try too hard. That's been my life's theme.

But Nadia presses me. "Why not?"

"I'm not lead singer material."

"Flynn, you know most of that crowd is there for you now, don't you?"

Something uncomfortable shifts through my mid-section.

"Those are girls," I say, like those fans don't count.

"So?"

"So, they're not obsessed with my talent, they're obsessed with some idea they have about me." I flash a grin her way. "They think I'm hot." I wink.

"You are hot." Her return smile gets my dick hard. This whole idea of knowing Nadia and I are going to have sex sometime soon makes it very difficult to have the "just friends" feeling around her. I may or may not have spent extra time in the shower this afternoon jacking off, so I could get sex off my mind. Even so, I have to work hard not to remember how fucking perfect she looked in nothing but her panties.

I hadn't absorbed it during the moment because she was upset, but that didn't mean the image of her glory hadn't been seared on my eyeballs. In my brain. There for me to pull out every night and every morning as I lay in bed with my dick in my hand. She had pale skin, peach-pink nipples, and a red birthmark on her hip. Her breasts were ripe peaches, her belly soft.

There's room in the parking lot when we get there. "The show doesn't start until nine, but I thought we could go in now, so you can meet the performers. Then we can grab some food and come back to watch the show if you want."

Nadia draws in a breath and nods. "Sounds good."

We head inside. Rue's is a small venue—an old Chicago building with exposed brick walls and lofted ceilings. The dancers are on the stage marking their places for a dance. There's no one at the door yet, and Rue, the owner, is behind the bar, her blue mohawk making her a good six inches taller.

"What's up, Flynn?" she calls out.

I love Rue. The middle-aged bar owner has the mama hen vibe to everyone who comes into her place. Her support in the way of rehearsal space and a standing gig was what got The Storytellers going. Rue's was also the only bar Ty, Lake, and I could get in before I turned twenty-one because Rue would vouch that we were in the band, even if it wasn't a night we played.

Consequently, I know all the regulars and staff here.

The burlesque night is more her scene because she's been in a long-term relationship with Danica, the director of the Black Velvet Burlesque troupe for as long as I've known her.

"What are you up to?" she asks when I lead Nadia to the bar.

Her hand is clammy this time, but the place is mostly empty, so I'm thinking she can work through it.

"I brought Nadia down to meet Danica. Nadia designs costumes. I thought maybe they could collaborate on something."

"Oh, sure." Rue sets a cocktail napkin in front of each of us. "What are you drinking?"

"Just a bottle of water for me for now," I say. "We'll be back to see the show later."

"Water is fine for me, too," Nadia says.

Rue grins. "Another Russian? I love my Saturday night Russian contingent. I always feel safer when Oleg is around."

"Yes, he's fearsome," I agree.

Nadia smiles and nods.

"I would ask him if he wants to moonlight as a bouncer when you lot play, but I figure he's already doing the job for free." Rue cracks two bottles of water and puts them on our napkins, and I toss a five-dollar bill on the bar.

"Right."

Music starts up, and the dancers take their places. Nadia and I swivel in our seats to watch. It's a sexy piece with a Cabaret vibe that involves giant feather fans the dancers use to cover various body parts as their clothes gradually come off. The clothes stay on for now, since it's just a run-through, but we get the general idea.

Nadia is enthralled. I watch her, checking to see if the sexual nature of it triggers her, but it seems to be the opposite. Her eyes shine with delight, and a smile plays around her lips.

When they're finished with their dress rehearsal, they come over to greet us.

"Flynn!" Amy, one of the members who—full disclosure—I've hooked up with, calls out, waving as she comes over. She isn't the only one I've had sex with. There's also Rebecca. And I haven't hooked up with Jane, but the vibe is there.

Nadia tenses as they approach, but her breath remains normal. I get hugs from Amy and Rebecca. Jane gives Nadia a nasty look.

"Ladies! This is Nadia. She's a fashion designer from Russia. She's interested in designing something for your show."

"I would not charge you," Nadia hurries to say. "It would just be fun for me to have a project for my portfolio."

"Oh my God, really?" Amy gushes. She's so close she's practically sitting on my lap, which I notice is pissing Nadia off, so I give her a little shove away.

"Hi, I'm Danica," their leader says, holding her hand out.

"Nadia." She shakes her hand.

"We'd definitely be interested. We don't really have a budget for costumes. Most of the dancers put together their own stuff."

"I understand. It would be free. Just a project for me."

"Then, you're hired." Danica gives her a smile.

"Wow." Nadia looks at me with big eyes then back at Danica. "That was easy. Thank you."

"Thank you. What do you need from us?"

"Nothing yet. I'm going to watch your show tonight, and then I'll start on some drawings."

Danica grabs a cocktail napkin and writes her phone number on it. "This is my number. You can text me or just come back here on a Thursday."

"Sounds great. Thank you!"

Amy moves back into my personal space, seemingly oblivious to my disinterest.

I stand to avoid having her try to perch on my lap again. "We'll be back to watch the show in a couple of hours," I say.

Nadia slides off her barstool, and I settle my hand on her back to lead her out. As soon as we're outside, she demands, "Okay, Flynn, how many?"

NADIA

I'm not jealous, I'm not jealous, I'm not jealous.

I had to tell myself that a hundred times in there.

"What?" Flynn asks innocently as he leads me to the street, but I know he already knows what I'm asking. He carries a guilty vibe I sort of hate.

I don't want to make him feel guilty. And I definitely don't want to be like every other girl who gets needy of his attention.

So I force some fake laughter out of my throat. "How many of those girls have you screwed?"

"Two," he answers.

"Only two? Which ones?"

"Amy, the one who was trying to sit on my lap, and Rebecca, the redhead giving you the evil eye."

"What about the pixie cut giving me the evil eye?"

"Well, she was going to be next." Flynn flashes me his apologetic grin, and I melt despite my resolve to not fall in love.

"She's cute." I try to be objective.

The truth is, I hate her. With a passion.

On the bright side, my jealousy and irritation completely grounded me in there. At no point was I freaked out, even with everyone standing too close. We're walking down the busy sidewalk now, passing people. There are cars zooming by, but none of it seems to be a trigger. I'm with Flynn. I'm fine.

"I'm sorry, did it bother you? Maybe I should've given you a heads up?"

I give a jerky shrug. "Of course not. We're friends, remember?"

"Yeah, but friends don't hurt each other's feelings."

"You didn't hurt my feelings," I say immediately. I don't want to be the kind of girl Flynn runs from. I want to be the one he gets to keep. As a friend, of course.

"I mean, you can have sex with whoever you want. With all of them."

He frowns, like he doesn't like me playing it cool. "Well, you're also my sex partner for the night—I mean, if you want—so I don't need you to play wingman for me."

I imagine I hear a trace of irritation in his voice—like he's annoyed that I'm not more jealous. But that wouldn't make sense.

"Sorry? I didn't think I was."

He *is* annoyed. I can tell by the little furrow between his brows. He pulls me into an alley and crowds me up against a brick wall. I'm not afraid. Not triggered. I sort of love seeing this side of Flynn. The easy-going swagger is gone.

This version of Flynn seems hungry. A little mad. His hands are on my waist. His lips find my neck, and he bites the skin there.

Still not triggered.

"What are you doing?" I laugh breathlessly.

"I want you riding my dick. Tonight. Tomorrow night. I want to give it to you so good you fight the other girls off me."

I let out a shocked laugh. "I thought you don't like clingy."

"You're not clingy. You're you. And I want you to want me." His open mouth drags across the column of my throat. "I want you to want me so badly you forget everything else. Every shitty thing that ever happened to you."

Not even his reminder of my imprisonment brings any of the sickness or fear back.

"Let's go," I say.

He pulls back to look at my face with a question.

"Show me your magic dick."

He laughs. "Come to my place?"

"Yes," I say immediately. I think this could be a *get back*

87

on the horse right away thing. I would feel so much better if I just knew I could do it. That I'm not completely broken.

Flynn grabs my hand and tugs me back to the street in the direction of the van, running a little, like hopping in his bed is an emergency.

And it is.

Flynn Taylor is going to reinvent me tonight. I'm absolutely sure of it.

CHAPTER 7

Flynn

I should go slowly.

I should be careful. Watch for signs of discomfort.

I know all these things, but they go out the window.

All I care about is getting Nadia out of her goddamn clothes and into my bed. I strip her on the way from my front door to the bedroom, devouring her mouth as I walk her backward. She strips me back, yanking up my shirt, and unbuckling my belt.

I manage to turn on a lamp in my bedroom. I cleaned up before our date, so the place is presentable.

Her kisses are demanding and greedy—what I wanted from her back at Rue's.

It was weird how reverse-jealous I got when she wasn't jealous over me. I'm so used to girls freaking over their competition. Getting territorial and staking their claim. I think it hurt my manly pride when Nadia didn't stake a claim.

Of course, she wouldn't. We are friends with benefits.

But I was surprised how badly I wanted her to. How offended I was by the notion that she wanted to share me.

I don't want to share her.

I seriously think I'd throat punch any guy who got near her, including Maykl, the huge bratva door guy she came to my show with that one time.

I push her up against the wall in my room and flick open the front clasp on her black bra. "I've been fucking my fist thinking about these tits for a week now," I groan when they spring free. "These are peaches," I assert.

Mental note—I need to buy her peaches so she knows what the hell I'm talking about.

I cup her breast and thumb over her nipple while my other hand tangles in her hair, holding her head still for more hot kisses. I love her butterscotch scent, the scratch of her fingernails on the back of my neck.

I can't think of the last time I've been this impassioned for a woman. I've had a lot of drunk sex that feels sort of desperate, but this is different. This is drunk-on-pheromones passion. I need more—no, *all*—of Nadia, or I will die.

She grinds down on my knee between her legs.

I shove a hand into her panties, sucking on the place behind her jaw as I gently part her flesh. She's wet and slick, and she jolts when I touch her clit.

I drop to my knees, yanking her pants and panties off as I go. Without waiting, as if my life depended on making this girl come in the next twenty seconds, I lift one of her knees and suck a spot on her inner thigh then fill my mouth with her juicy pussy. There's no finesse. No delicate tracing with my tongue. I suck, lick and nip every inch of her feminine folds. I penetrate her with my tongue, penetrate her with two fingers. With her leg hooked over my shoulder, I give her every ounce of passion I know, all designed to make her feel good.

"Flynn...Flynn." She yanks off my knit cap and tears at my hair, pressing my face against her for more.

I lash her with my tongue as I locate her g-spot with my two fingers, finding the place where the tissue stiffens and raises under my fingers. I pump in and out, hitting it every time, while I lap and flick and suck at her clit.

She clenches around my fingers with a shriek.

Without giving her time to recover, I rise up and pick her up to straddle my waist, carrying her to the bed.

"I want you to come all over my dick this time. Are you going to do that for me?" I ask, toeing off my shoes and shoving my pants off.

"*Da.* Yes. I will," she promises, her hands traveling over my shoulders and down my biceps.

Wanting her to feel in control, I roll the condom over my dick as I lie down. "Climb on, Peaches."

NADIA

I'm doing this. I'm totally in the moment. Totally with Flynn, who is carrying me away with his unbridled passion.

Cigar guy isn't here in the room. He's not between us.

I straddle Flynn's waist and position my entrance over his cock. He holds the base steady for me as I rise up and slowly lower over him. I love that he put me in charge. I get to control this. I'm on top. I have space. I can breathe. I can pace things the way I need them to be paced.

I definitely feel safe.

More than that–I feel alive. Lit up. Tingling with excitement.

Flynn's groan echoes off the walls when I take him inside me. "You're killing me, Peaches. You feel so good."

My hands fall to his sturdy shoulders, my hair falls across my face. I catch my lip between my teeth as I ride him. He grips my ass to help, pulling me on and off, meeting my rhythm with upward thrusts of his own.

It feels so good. I had no idea how good this could feel. I cry out and throw my head back, my breasts bouncing as I take his cock deeper.

"That's it, Nadia. Take what you need from me."

My pussy gushes lubrication. My nails score Flynn's skin as I ride him faster, like we're in a race to the finish line. Breath rasping, teeth clenched, a wild determination fuels my movements.

"*Da...Da,*" I cry, forgetting which language to speak.

"Take it, Nadia," Flynn encourages, giving me all the power. Making this all about my pleasure. My enjoyment. "Use me to get where you need to go."

"I will," I pant, "I will! *Gospodi,* yes!"

My movements grow erratic, and I babble in Russian then scream. My internal muscles squeeze and pulse around his dick.

He thrusts up into me, seeking his own pleasure now that I've found mine. "Yes, Nadia. Fuck, yeah." Lights dance before my eyes when he comes. The room gets hot. It spins a little.

And when my vision clears, my face breaks into the biggest smile possible.

I'm totally triumphant.

I must be glowing.

Flynn pulls me down for a kiss, and that's when I know: I couldn't have screwed this up more.

Because I don't want Flynn as a friend.

Not at all.

I want everything from him.

Heart. Body. Soul.

I'm flying like one of those kites people carry along the shore of Lake Michigan. Buoyant. Aloft. Flapping and fluttering in the wind.

I'm a new woman. Capable of being intimate with a man. Capable of orgasming–twice!

I feel like I just won a race. Or the lottery. Like I completed some spectacular feat that I never thought could happen for me.

I straddle Flynn's hips and smile down at him. "I did it."

He smiles back. "You did. We did. You're beautiful."

He makes me feel beautiful. More importantly, I don't feel frightened over him finding me beautiful. I don't want to disengage from my body.

"I'm so happy." It's an understatement. I'm downright ecstatic.

Flynn holds my hips and undulates his beneath me a few times, with satisfying, unambitious thrusts.

I climb off him, pull on my panties, and flit about his room on shaking legs.

I just had sex. I just orgasmed. I swear to God, I didn't even know if it would ever be possible to feel sexual pleasure again, but I did it!

I investigate everything in his room, wanting to absorb all that is Flynn. Wanting to somehow hang onto and keep this sense of happiness that's overcome me.

It's a guy room. An acoustic guitar stands in the corner. A blown glass pipe for smoking weed is on the dresser, along with a library card and a Starbucks gift card.

I open his closet and investigate his clothing.

"Are you going to style me?" He rolls his lanky form off the bed and disposes of the condom.

"Will you let me?"

His chuckle is warm and rusty. It ignites tiny explosions under my ribs. "Sure. Yeah. Of course."

So easy.

Everything with Flynn is always so easy. There's no pressure. There's no agenda.

Even when things got heated during sex, he was so damn *present* with me. His passion carried me along. Or ignited mine.

I examine the clothes in his closet. Mostly button-down shirts—not the expensive crisp ones that Ravil or Maxim wear, but worn flannels and just a couple dress shirts. He has a few pairs of dress slacks. I open his dresser drawers and peek inside. They are packed with more comfortable shirts and pullovers, jeans and khakis.

Flynn pulls a pair of boxer briefs on and picks up the guitar, folding his long body into a cross-legged position on the bed. He starts to play. The lamplight falls across his face, lighting his boyish good looks. This could be a music video—Flynn shirtless and happy, hanging out playing music in the bed where he just made love.

In fact…

"Hang on." I pull a pair of flannel pajama pants out of his dresser. "Put these on."

"Okay." He doesn't ask me why. He doesn't protest. He just climbs off the bed to put on the pants. "Now what?"

I turn on another lamp. "Go back to the bed and play."

He leans over and brushes his lips across the bridge of my nose. "I like you bossy."

I laugh. "I'm not bossy. I just have an idea."

"What is it?"

"You just play the guitar, like you were."

I find his phone where he dropped it with his keys and

open up the Tiktok app. Flynn has a profile there. I know because I follow him. He doesn't post that often–usually just clips from their live shows–but he has a decent following because of Skate 32's videos and the Storyteller's growing local fanbase.

I take a seat in the armchair by the window and go live.

"What are you doing?" His eyes crinkle when he smiles at me as his fingers dance over the strings. The guy can play anything without ever making it seem hard.

"I'm live streaming the megastar Flynn Taylor from his bedroom."

He sends me a lazy grin. "Yeah?"

"Mmm hmm. I think your fans would love to see you like this."

He looks beautiful. Like a rock god–shirtless with an armband tattoo around his sculpted biceps. Hair mussed. Totally into his music.

He plucks a tune I don't recognize.

"What's that?"

"It's how I feel with you." His eyes crinkle again and flutters start up in my stomach.

The part that gets me–beyond just how incredibly sexy he looks right now in the lamplight–is that the song isn't sad. The tune that he's playing for me is light and easy. Full of possibilities.

"That's how I feel with you," I counter.

He flashes another grin and starts humming softly, swaying his shoulders a bit. I'm ready to come again just watching him. Knowing the music is about me.

His phone shows a DM come through from Cadence. *I see you on Tiktok! Where are you tonight? Can I come over?*

I don't mean to–oh, who am I kidding? I totally mean to–open up their chat window. He's received seven messages from her but hasn't responded to a single one. No reason for me to feel threatened. I'm the one in his bedroom.

I go back to watching the Tiktok screen. We already have 106 viewers, and the comments are coming in.

Who is filming?

Who's the girl?

I love you Flynn!

They scroll up the screen.

I'm not jealous. Not this time. Not when Flynn just gave me everything. Maybe later, I will be when I contemplate how easily unattached Flynn always seems. When I remember that I don't get to keep him. That he could be with another girl tomorrow night. But right now, I feel honored to be the girl in his bedroom. Honored enough to want to share him with the world. Help him get famous.

Because Flynn definitely deserves to have it all. He has crazy talent and remains so humble. So friendly and go-lucky. Flynn doesn't feel the need to perform, even though he knows I'm streaming him. He plays around–trying out different tunes, strumming chords, going back to the first melody.

Everyone watching is getting to see a musician's real process, and it's absolutely beautiful.

The number of viewers grows to 356. Then 482. Then 789.

Maybe they aren't huge numbers compared to some Tiktok stars, but I bet if Flynn did this regularly, he'd get a huge following.

"Is this the way you write your songs?" I ask.

He flashes that pirate smile at me. "Yeah, I guess. It's been a while since I've composed anything."

"Is it hard?"

He gives a chuckle. "It's really easy. Or else it's super hard. Seems like the harder you try, the harder it is. If you don't really care whether you write a song or not, that's when music just pours out of you."

"Mmm. You need to be in the zone," I say.

"Yeah, I guess." Another panty-melting smile.

I draw my feet up on the armchair and prop the phone on one knee.

Who is the Russian? someone asks, hearing my accent.

Is that your girlfriend? Jelly! another posts.

I hate her. Get out of Flynn's room, slut.

I love the new song.

I ignore the nasty remarks from his fangirls. I expected them. I've already seen how competitive they get at his shows. Discouraging them would be wrong, even if their vitriol makes my stomach churn. It's girls like this who will ultimately get the Storytellers noticed. Maybe signed to a major label.

Flynn plays a while longer then stops and sets the guitar beside him. "Are you hungry?"

"I could eat," I say. I'm still filming. Maybe I'm crazy, but I think every single thing Flynn does ought to be absorbed by his fans. Adored the way I adore him.

He walks toward me, a beautiful, glorious lion. Lanky and lean, but still muscled with a light dusting of golden hair on his chest. He leans down and kisses me.

I pan up from his abs to his face before I end the video. He had 10,472 views.

"Is this my new style? Pajama pants?" he teases.

"For this particular moment, yes. It's a very good look for you."

"You didn't want me in my underwear?"

"That might get you banned. Also, I don't want every-one–" I stop because I sound territorial. Like his middle school girlfriend. I don't want to do that.

He grabs my wrist and tugs me to my feet. His smirk

makes my nipples harden. Or maybe it's just his nearness. "You don't want everyone to see me in my underwear?"

My face grows warm. "No, it's all right. I know we're not—"

"Shut up, Nadia." He grasps the back of my head and kisses me, hard. It's more aggressive than usual, but I like it.

Scratch that—I love it.

I needed Flynn to be easy-going and non-threatening before. Now I need the passion. I want to know it's me he wants. That I turn him on. That I'm not replaceable.

Except I am replaceable, aren't I? I set this whole thing up that way.

"I wouldn't want anyone to see you in just your underwear, either." He traces the tip of his finger along the waistband of my panties, making my tummy shiver at his touch.

He kisses me again, this time gripping a handful of my ass and squeezing. My erect nipples rub against his ribs, and moisture slicks my lady parts again.

"How badly do you want to see the burlesque show?" Flynn asks between kisses. "Because I could skip dinner and just eat you again."

It sounds heavenly, but I want both. I gently push him away, and he immediately backs off—ever respectful. "I want to go," I tell him.

"Then we'll go," he says easily.

"I haven't been out in so long, and you make it all feel possible. Not just possible—fun."

"It will be fun." He stoops to pick up my pants and tosses them my way.

"Plus, I want the dancers to take me seriously. I already have ideas for their costumes."

"Trust me—they will be overjoyed to have your help.

Artists jump at the chance to get something for free. We're always starving, you know." He winks at me.

"Are you?" I stop, shocked. I didn't know.

"No, no, no. It's cool. We're starting to make money, actually, which I never expected."

"But not a lot." I suddenly want to help him, too. I have that money from Kat's dad. Maybe I could put it to good use with him and the band.

"The point was never to make money." There's a line between Flynn's brows I don't like seeing.

"But wouldn't it be great if you did?" I challenge. Something about his self-deprecation that feels wrong here.

He shrugs. "I don't want to chase fame." He holds my jacket out for me, like a gentleman. I didn't even know boys our age knew how to do that. I try to resist the yearning kicking up inside me. The desire to have Flynn for keeps. For always.

It's not going to happen, and I shouldn't start wanting it now. Instead I press him on the fame issue. "Why not?"

He puts his jacket on, picks up his phone and keys and leads me out of the apartment. "My dad was always waiting to get discovered, and then one day, he just became kind of bitter, you know? I never wanted to be like that. The Storytellers are for fun. Because I can't live without music. And it is my livelihood, too, but…"

I peer up at him as we go down the stairs. "You can't avoid dreams just because you're afraid they won't come true," I tell him. I see his customary smile fade, and I'm sorry I'm the one who dimmed his light. "Sorry," I say when he doesn't answer.

"No, it's cool. I see what you mean. I'm just not sure I want to go that route."

"The having dreams route?"

"Yeah."

"What if you're pushing away success right now just because you're afraid of it?" I sound like some kind of life coach–which isn't me, but it just seems too clear that's what he's doing. I've been working with a therapist for months now–I guess she's starting to rub off on me.

Flynn stops on the sidewalk outside and loops an arm behind my back. He draws me up against him. Our breaths mingle in the cold air. "You make me want to believe," he murmurs and kisses me.

"I believe anything's possible when I'm with you," I whisper back.

CHAPTER 8

Nadia

I'm in love. I want to be a burlesque dancer. They are everything.

I watch the way the women hold their own on the stage. They dominate. They are sexual—

but empowered. Beautiful and demanding of our attention.

This is exactly what I need. This energy. Taking back my sexuality. Giving it on my terms.

I want to be up on that stage deciding exactly how much skin I show. Giving access to my body on my own terms.

Owning the audience.

We sit at a table sipping soda water with lime and dropping dollar bills in the dancers' buckets when they sweep through the audience requesting tips.

Flynn drapes a casual arm across the back of my chair and keeps glancing over, like he's more interested in what I think than the actual show. For a guy who doesn't do commitment or girlfriends, he's so damn attentive.

He always seems to have his finger on my pulse, knowing what I need. When I'm starting to freak out and when I'm having fun.

~

Flynn

I study Nadia's profile as we sit at a table at Rue's to watch the show. I've seen the show before—or many variations of it. I used to work at Rue's taking the cover charge at the door a few nights a week.

Watching Nadia take it in is far more entertaining. The dancers are on stage doing a group dance. Tonight they are a troupe of five women and one drag queen, but it varies week to week. They have individual pieces and a few group pieces. Their art involves lip sync, dance, strip tease and performance art. They're not super polished, but it doesn't matter—it's their raw presence that makes the crowd love them. That and the sexual nature of the show.

Nadia clearly loves everything she sees. Her expression is rapt and full of light. She radiates pleasure and life.

I'm in love.

Wow. First time for everything, right?

I mean, this has to be love. The way I feel with Nadia is like nothing I've experienced before. She makes me feel like a different person. A better version of myself.

I don't want to drink or smoke around her.

I want to write songs.

Now she has me thinking I might even man up and put some effort into making the band into more.

After driving back to Rue's neighborhood, we stopped in at a pizza joint to fill our bellies then came in here to get a table. I ordered a Coke and Nadia's drinking Sprite. She said she shouldn't drink because she's on anti-anxiety meds. I don't have any urge to touch alcohol or weed around her.

I feel the need to stay sober around Nadia. It's not just because I feel protective but also just because I don't want to miss anything. Not a single nuance or word she utters. I want to absorb it all. She is light and unicorns. And yes, sometimes puddles, but I would take a thousand rain showers and mud puddles and punches in the jaw for a night like this.

The dance ends, and she cheers, looking at me to see if I'm as enthusiastic as she is. "I love it," she tells me. "I want to join them."

"What?" I lean forward to make sure I heard that right.

"I want to join them. I want to be a burlesque dancer."

I absorb that. It makes sense. The dancers own and control their own sexuality. They're on stage. They're in charge. In control. After what Nadia's been through, it makes sense that she'd crave that sense of ownership and control over her body and how it is viewed.

"Awesome," I say, determined to make sure it happens. Even if it means talking her through a dozen panic attacks to get her there, I will make sure she gets on that stage if she wants to.

"Do you think I could?"

"I'm sure you could," I say. I'll help make it happen if she needs me, but I have little doubt she could arrange it all on her own. All she needs is a little encouragement and a nudge. "Talk to Danica. Maybe they have classes or something."

She nods. "When I show her my costume ideas I will ask her."

"Perfect," I agree.

I can't imagine it wouldn't work out—so long as Nadia

doesn't have a panic attack on stage. But I would be with her to make sure it didn't happen.

As I contemplate all the untapped potential lurking within Nadia, I suddenly understand what she meant about me blocking my own success.

If I believe she can do anything she wants to—and I do—why wouldn't I believe the same of myself? I haven't done much with my life, but it doesn't mean I can't. Nadia sees potential in me, which is more than I see in myself.

"Let's go back to your place." Nadia's lips at my ear. She's turned on by the show. I love it. I didn't expect her to want to return to my place, but I'm down. I'm more than down. I'm freaking ready.

I throw a tip on the table and stand up, grabbing her hand. Her smile is wide as I lead her out the door. We jog for the van, just like we did last time. Like we can't wait to get our hands on each other again. I am definitely in love.

Totally and completely in love.

NADIA

"You sit here." I point to the armchair in the middle of Flynn's living room. I want to do a striptease. I want to be like those women on stage tonight. Sultry and seductive. Holding all the power.

Flynn drops into the chair, his eyes darkened with desire.

"I need stripping music," I tell him.

He calls up "Sexy Back" on his phone, and it starts playing through a speaker in the kitchen.

I prance around the room finding the beat. I stop and swing my hips, sinking to a squat, then rising again.

Flynn groans in approval, his thumb resting on his lower lip.

I remove my clothing piece by piece until I'm in nothing but my panties. Some of my moves are sexy. Some are silly. It doesn't matter because Flynn appears to be enthralled by everything I do. At the end of the song, I straddle his waist, undulating my hips over his hardened cock.

I lower to my knees at his feet and unbutton his pants. His manhood bulges against the thin fabric of his boxer briefs. I free his erection and fist it. I'm going to give him the best blowjob I know how.

I open my lips, but as my mouth gets close, unwanted memories flood my mind. Fear makes my muscles seize. My throat closes. The mechanical whirring of gears clangs and rattles in my ears.

I jerk back, suddenly that other girl–the broken one.

I'm going to be sick.

I run for the bathroom.

"Nadia?" Flynn charges after me, his voice laced with concern, which only makes it worse.

I shut the bathroom door, trying to lock it, but he twists the handle before I do. I jump back as it flies open.

"I'm sorry." I shake all over. My body's in trauma, even though my mind wants to stay with Flynn.

"Hey," he says softly, stepping into the small space with me. "It's okay." He opens his arms but doesn't make any demands.

I was ready to crouch in the corner and hide, embarrassed over my breakdown, but it seems so much simpler to just enter the circle of his embrace.

When I do, he tightens his arms around me. "You don't have to run and hide from me." He rocks from foot to foot, slow dancing with me around the bathroom, his lips on my hair. "We're in this together."

I let out a rough sob.

"I signed up for this, remember? I knew it wouldn't be easy."

"It was earlier," I complain.

"Yeah. And this time it wasn't. That's okay, too." He massages the back of my neck.

"I wanted to…" I can't even talk about giving head. The memory of being repeatedly forced is too much in the forefront of my brain.

"It's cool. Everything's fine, Peaches. Let's go to bed. Are you staying the night?"

Am I? I didn't think that far ahead. Tonight, I've blissfully lived moment by moment, and they were all great until now.

But Flynn's inviting me to spend the night with him.

Flynn Taylor, the guy who doesn't do girlfriends. The king of casual sex. The unrepentant player.

He wants me in his bed tonight. And not for sex.

I lift my head and nod.

"Want a toothbrush?" He opens a cabinet below the sink and produces one still in the package.

I give him a weak smile. "Thank you."

He just gives me that easy grin and puts a line of toothpaste on his toothbrush then mine. We stand at the sink and brush our teeth together like an old married couple.

It feels easy. The trauma starts to slip off me, like a jacket I can take off when I come inside from the cold. My heartbeat calms. The sweating in my palms goes away. I still feel queasy, but I try not to think about it.

I watch Flynn brush his teeth, his muscles flexing against his shirt. He makes even the most ordinary action look sexy.

We both spit and rinse our mouths out, and Flynn heads to the bedroom while I use the toilet. When I get to the bedroom, the lights are off. He has the covers open, and he's lying in bed propped on one elbow, waiting for me.

I climb in beside him, and he rolls to wrap an arm around my waist. For a while, I listen to the sound of his breath, wondering what he thinks about me now. He didn't seem disappointed. I think I'm more disappointed than he is.

As if in answer to my wondering, he murmurs, "You're strong, Nadia. And brave. You will shake this."

I roll over in the dark and rest my head on his shoulder. "I was drugged most of time," I tell him, my accent thicker with emotion.

It seems easier to talk about it in the dark. I can almost smell the nauseating scent of cigar smoke, but I inhale Flynn's scent instead.

"It was–how do you say it in English–a blessing and a curse. Both."

"Yeah?"

"Blessing because my memories are all fuzzy. I can almost pretend it was nightmare–not real."

Flynn strokes my cheek but otherwise doesn't respond, leaving the space open for me to go on.

"It's a curse because when they do surface, I get confused and scared. I have a strong reaction."

Flynn makes a rumbling sound.

"It took my brain chemistry a long time to adjust after I got free. Some of my depression was chemical. I wanted to scrub my brain of all of it, you know?"

"Yeah."

"But when you asked me to go to a party with you, I

asked for the anti-anxiety medication my therapist wanted me to try. And it does help."

"There's no shame in using medication, for the time being or permanently. Whatever it takes for you to regain your life, Nadia."

I nestle closer to him. "You're so wise for your age. Why is that?"

"My mom struggles with mental illness. She was hospitalized a lot when I was growing up... for depression."

"*Gospodi*, that must have been hard. I'm sorry."

I feel him shrug beneath my head. "It was all right. There was a lot of love. Our family was crazy and chaotic, but we took good care of each other. Story took care of me and Dahlia when our mom couldn't function."

"Dahlia is the sister in Wisconsin?"

"Yes. She and her high school boyfriend went together and are still making it work. She turned out the most normal of all of us."

Hearing Flynn's warm rumble sloughs away more of the residual trauma in my body.

"Adrian had to look out for me, too. Our mom died of cancer, and our dad became an alcoholic."

"That's why it's hard for him to take a step back now."

"*Da*. Also...My kidnapping changed him. A lot. It made him feel helpless, and now he overcompensates. He had to become something else in order to get me back."

"A member of the Russian *mafiya*."

"*Da*. He has blood on his hands now."

"Yeah. I'm sure Oleg does, too. Probably way more."

"Does it bother you? Your sister being engaged to a bratva member?"

"Honestly? No. That guy is one hundred percent a teddy bear with her. I guess my only worry would be that something bad would happen to him, and she'd be left alone."

We're quiet a while longer. The mechanical gear sounds stop completely. The anxiety of trying to make it all go away isn't here, either. For the first time, I actually feel brave enough to try to look at what triggered me.

Forced oral sex. That was it.

"There was a guy who came every night. The same guy," I tell Flynn. I feel like puking, but it's not worth holding it in. Keeping these stories inside me is what makes them too much to manage.

Flynn goes still.

"He smelled like cigars and liked the rape thing. Even though I was chained, he still had to hold me down or choke me. And he always used *me*. I was his… don't know—preferred slave. He liked to gag me with his…" I trail off because now I really don't want to finish the story.

Flynn says nothing, but there's more tension in him than usual. I don't sense the same spacious allowance he usually offers.

After a moment, he says, "I get why Adrian is the way he is. I'm not violent, but I would definitely kill that guy if I had the chance."

"Me too," I murmur. And it's true.

Adrian was hunting the leader of the sex trafficking ring—Kat's father. I didn't care about him. I never met him.

The man I want dead is the *mudak* who haunts my nightmares. Maybe in the law's eyes, he's the least culpable. He wasn't selling me. He was just buying. I don't care—he's the one I remember most. He's the one who actually raped me—over and over again. And after what he did to me, he doesn't deserve to live.

"So he's still alive? Adrian didn't get to him?"

The whirring gears start up, but I don't resist. I let

them play in my head. A soundtrack to my torment. Except this time, I recognize the torment as something different than victimhood. This time it feels like rage.

"*Nyet.* I would like to find him. And if I did, I would put gun to his head and pull the trigger myself." I feel sick saying it, but there's also something steadying about admitting my desire for violence.

"I'd bury the body for you," Flynn says.

I feel laughter somewhere in my chest. It doesn't come out. It feels far away, and yet it registers enough to lighten my mood. I throw my leg over Adrian's hips. "Would you?"

I suspect we're playing Flynn's storyteller game right now. Concocting a story that would never happen but is fun to imagine. It's strange pillow talk, yet I've never felt closer to another person in my life. This conversation is exactly what I needed.

"I'd drive the getaway car. I'd tie him up and hold him in place. But only if you're a good shot." There's teasing in Flynn's voice, as if he sensed my shift in mood.

"I'm not," I admit. "I actually don't know how to shoot a gun. So you'd better not hold him in place in case I screw it up."

"I would beat the shit out of him first, so he was incapable of moving, and then you could shoot him."

I try to picture it. It's really too absurd to imagine. I could see Adrian doing it. Or any of his bratva brothers, but me and Flynn? It feels as fantastical as it sounds. I like to pretend, though. "I would like to pull the trigger. I think I could."

"If you couldn't, I would finish it for you."

Pressure lifts off me in rolling waves. I'm me again. Not that lost, broken me, but the real me. Solid. Grounded. Built of sturdy bones and covered in peaches and cream skin.

I want to thank Flynn. I also want to try again. To erase the presence of the cigar man in the room. In our sex life. Under my skin.

I crawl down under the covers, straddling Flynn's legs.

"You don't have to, Nadia. I don't care if my dick gets sucked or not. I'm good." He reaches for me. "Let me taste you."

"I want to." I fist his cock, which instantly firms in my grip. "I really need to do this."

"Turn around, then," Flynn urges. "Sixty-nine. Sit on my face."

I laugh because it's not something I've ever tried.

I'd had sex before I was enslaved. A few boyfriends. But I guess there's still a lot I don't know. Flynn probably knows everything.

It's embarrassing, but I change position, kneeling over his face. Even though it's dark, I squeeze my eyes shut tight, willing the memories back, chanting in my head, *This is Flynn, this is Flynn, this is Flynn.*

He grips my thighs and tugs me down to his mouth, his tongue parting my flesh. I moan at the contact. My clit is already sensitized from our earlier round, and my ass jerks at the zing of sensation that shoots straight to my core.

Flynn works me with enthusiasm, sucking at my labia, tonguing me in at least five different ways. It makes it easy to surrender to the sensation. To forget the thing I'm most afraid of—my past overtaking the present.

It's easy to open my mouth and take the head of Flynn's cock into the pocket of my cheek. As I grow more confident, more secure, I angle it straight back. I'm on top. I'm in control. No one will choke me. This is for Flynn.

This is also for me.

My pleasure matches his. Giving and receiving at the same time.

I sink into the moment. There isn't the desperate edge to reach a finish line that we had before. There isn't even a proving to myself that I can do this.

I'm already doing it. I already have done it.

There's no pressure to perform. I can actually slow down and enjoy. I take my time, licking around the head of Flynn's cock, flicking my tongue along the slit. When I take him deep into my mouth again, he groans against my flesh and starts licking with more animation.

Happiness slips in.

A slice of glory.

I haven't orgasmed yet, but the feel-good hormones have already rushed to my brain, bathing it in pleasure. Love. Bonding.

"Nadia?" Flynn's voice is deep and raspy with lust.

"*Da?*"

"Can I fuck you, babe? I want to get on top and fuck you good."

"Yes," I breathe. "*Pozhaluysta*...please." I scramble off him and turn around on the bed.

He gets up on his knees and meets me in the middle, looping an arm behind my back and kissing me with the gloss of my juices on his lips. "Just say no if it doesn't feel good, okay?"

I nod my head. I already know that won't happen. I'm so ready for him. I want to feel everything he wants to give me.

"Lie down on your belly, Peaches," he murmurs.

When I do, he grabs a pillow and lifts my hips to slip it under them. Then he climbs over me. "Spread your legs, sweetheart."

I hear the snap of a foil wrapper as he puts a condom on, then he stands on his knees between my thighs and lowers his body over mine. His cock nudges at my entrance. I tip my ass up to take him.

He goes slowly, but I'm so wet and ready, there's no resistance. Especially after our first session. He feeds his length into me, inch by inch until his loins hit my ass. The head of his cock strokes my inner walls in the perfect place.

It feels wonderful.

Perfect, even.

He blankets my body with his entire form, sliding an arm under my ribs, so he's holding me in an embrace as he snaps his hips to drive into me.

"I'm right here," he murmurs against my ear. "Are you good?"

"So good," I breathe, opening my legs even wider.

He nibbles along my neck, the seductive tenderness balancing out the animalistic force with which he fucks me. It's a little wild and rough but still very personal. Intimate. Our two bodies work in concert to drive us both to the precipice.

I start to cry out, and Flynn slows, brushing my hair back from my cheek to see my face.

"Don't stop," I moan. "Please. I need more. Please."

"I'll give it to you, sweetheart." He slides the hand underneath me down between our legs and finds my clit. One pinch, and I'm shrieking, hurtling over the edge into oblivion.

I shatter and come back together. Shatter again. I spin. No, the room spins—I float.

I'm flying, like the wish from the rainbow grasshopper was granted to me instead of Flynn.

Or maybe he's flying, too.

He hasn't finished yet, though. He waits until my muscles stop clenching and squeezing around his cock, and then he rises up on one arm to brace himself above me and pounds into me. "Are you okay?" he pants, still thinking about my comfort.

"*Da, da, da!*" I want him to come. To feel as glorious as I do.

And he does. He slams in deep with a shout and drops to hold me tight again.

Tears prick my eyes because it's so wonderful. It was so easy and wonderful and perfect.

I knew Flynn would be the guy.

But now, I don't know what to do.

Now, I'm completely lost.

Because I'm pretty sure I've fallen head over heels in love with this man.

The player.

The guy who doesn't want a girlfriend.

CHAPTER 9

Flynn

I wake to a loud, insistent banging on my door.

"Fuck," I groan, rolling out of bed.

Nadia sits up looking spectacularly tumbled. Her copper-lit hair falls in her face, her cheeks are still flushed with sleep. She gets up and pads to the bathroom.

I want to kill whoever the fuck is at my door.

Especially because Nadia woke up with a nightmare during the night and could use all the extra sleep she could get.

Having Nadia sleep in my bed last night gave me a new purpose in life: Nadia.

I'm serious.

It's like until this moment, I've just been drifting along. I was available to prop up my mom. I was a warm body in the band. But it's like something in me just woke up. Or activated.

Some essential coding within me got turned on.

But to say my new purpose is Nadia isn't quite right.

It's more like I was the lock and Nadia was the key. Now that she's turned me on, I'm available for myself, too.

I'm willing to put some effort into my life.

I suddenly see my past self so clearly—who I was and who I was unwilling to be.

And this is the real me—the person I was previously unwilling to be.

I know it sounds like I'm on a mushroom trip right now, but I'm not. I've never felt more sober or enlightened in my life. That's the other thing—I now see how my desire to party was a numbing mechanism. I used sex and drugs and alcohol to keep me from being my true self.

This man.

Because I'm capable of so much more, and I didn't want to try. To be it.

I was afraid of failing, I think.

But for Nadia, I would totally try.

Anything at all.

I hop on one foot as I pull on my boxer briefs. "Hang on." I call to Nadia in the bathroom, "I'll get rid of them. I'm sorry."

The thumping keeps pounding on the door. I close the bedroom door to give Nadia privacy and stomp to the front door. "What the fuck is your—" the word *problem* dies on my lips as Adrian pushes me aside to enter my apartment. Kat follows behind him, throwing me an apologetic look.

"Did you come to beat on me again?"

"Where is she?"

The toilet flushes, making the answer to his question obvious.

"Are you out of your fucking mind? Nadia is fine. She doesn't need you to rescue her from me."

Nadia emerges from my bedroom wearing—*oh God, she*

looks glorious!–one of my t-shirts. The vintage Ramones shirt hits her mid-thigh and makes her look good enough to eat.

"Adrian, what are you doing here?" She shoves her hair out of her face. Her voice is still laced with sleep, and I revel in the fact that she sounds happy. Like she just had the best night's rest.

Adrian narrows his eyes at her. "Why the fuck haven't you answered my texts?"

"Um, I think that's kind of obvious, Adrian," Kat says. To me and Nadia, she says, "We're sorry. We didn't mean to interrupt."

"How did you even find this place?" Nadia asks.

"I have a tracker on your phone," Adrian admits in a grumble. "For safety."

"Well, I'm safe." Nadia walks up behind me and wraps her arms around me. It's the kind of gesture I normally hate from a girl on the morning after–and I don't usually even do morning afters–but I absolutely love it this time. It feels like Nadia's claiming me–which she has refused to do before now. Like she wants to stay and not run off with her brother this time.

I lift one arm over her head to draw her against my side. "Please stay," I murmur. I sound like the clingy girls I try to avoid, but something about Nadia leaving today alarms me.

I want her with me, filling this apartment with her magical presence. I want to work on that song she inspired in me last night while I'm looking at her beautiful face.

Adrian tips his head toward the door. "Come on. I'll take you home."

"I'm going to stay," Nadia says, and I let out the breath I didn't realize I was holding.

"How long?"

"Bro," I cut in. "She's not a child. She has your

117

number if she needs anything, but she won't because I'm not going to fuck this up."

Nadia lifts her face to me in surprise. In fact, all three of them stare at me as if I've sprouted a banana tree from the top of my head, and I realize I've said way too much out loud.

Nadia and I are officially just friends. There shouldn't be anything to fuck up.

But it's out there, and I won't take it back.

"I have an extra rehearsal over there this afternoon. I can drive you home then," I offer.

Adrian gives me a long, hard look. "I don't trust you," he says finally.

Fuck.

"I do," Nadia pipes up. "I would trust Flynn to the ends of the Earth."

Adrian shakes his head. "Nadia..." He scrubs a hand across his face. "Do you know how many girls have been in his bed?"

Double fuck. I feel like I've been punched in the gut. Of course, there's nothing I can say to that because it's true.

This doesn't feel like the right time to make that confession to Nadia that I want something more than what we have. I wish to hell I'd done it last night before she fell asleep with her sweet head resting on my shoulder.

"Yes," Nadia says simply, chin lifted. "It doesn't matter or make him untrustworthy. It just means he's good in bed, which is what I need right now."

Ouch.

I'd like to think I brought more than sex to the table, but maybe I'm delusional. I mean, Nadia was honest from the start about what she wanted. A bed partner to help her have sex again.

I did that for her.

Maybe now is when we go back to being friends.

But no, she said she's staying.

Just for sex, a voice in my head grumbles. I know I should ask her. We need to have a conversation to clarify and redefine, except even as I think it, I know I probably won't do it. Because I don't want to end this prematurely.

If she only wants sex, but isn't finished yet, I want it to keep playing out.

I don't want her to end things because I declare myself in love with her.

Dammit. I'm in a fucking pickle here.

Well, for starters, I need her to stay and Adrian to leave. I focus on him. "I won't hurt Nadia. I understand what she's been through, and I'm careful. I'm paying attention. I know how to be the guy she needs."

Adrian considers me like he's seeing me for the first time.

Or like he sees the new me. The one Nadia revealed. "You have bigger balls than I expected," he admits.

"I won't hurt her," I repeat.

She may demolish me, but I would die before I hurt Nadia.

"If you do, I'll cut those nuts off and feed them to your—"

"*Oh*-kay," Kat interrupts loudly. "We're leaving. Bye. Love you, Nadia." She blows a kiss to Nadia with one hand as she tugs Adrian's elbow with the other.

Adrian doesn't move despite Kat's attempts. He points a tattooed finger at me.

"*Go*, Adrian," Nadia says.

Abruptly he turns, puts an arm around Kat and guides her out the door.

Nadia groans when the door shuts. "I'm sorry my brother is such an ass."

"It's cool," I say. I'm still smarting from the notion that I'm just a sex therapist for Nadia, but I don't plan to let it show.

She still has her arms around me from the side, and she peers up at me now. "Why are you so nice to me?"

I smile down at her, dazzled by her affection. "You're pretty good to me, too, Peaches."

"Am I?"

I nod, cupping the side of her face and kissing her forehead. I breathe in her butterscotch scent. "Really good. What do you want to do for breakfast?"

Excitement lights her face. "We could...um...go somewhere?"

I know it's a leap for her. Or a week ago it would've been. Now she's suggesting outings herself.

"Absolutely," I say immediately. "But there's something I need first."

"What is it?"

"Come here." I swivel and walk her backward until her ass hits the overstuffed arm of the sofa. I pick her up by the waist and sit her on it, then drop to my knees and spread her thighs.

"*Oy.*" I loved the shocked, pleased syllable that leaves her lips.

I delve my tongue between her folds, seeking that now-familiar taste. Exploring her delicate pleats with the tip of my tongue.

She grips my head to keep from falling back, shrieking and laughing a little. "Flynn....*da.*"

I work her into a frenzy with my tongue, then slip my thumb inside her as I push back the hood of her clitoris and suck the little bead between my lips.

She screams, her knees slapping against my shoulders as she comes around my thumb.

It occurs to me that any upright sexual position might be a win for her. If she was chained to a bed, she couldn't have been on her feet.

I rise and slip my thumb out. "Stay here. Don't move, okay, Peaches?"

She looks too dazed to go anywhere, anyway. She gives me a glassy-eyed nod, and I rush to the bedroom to grab a condom. Her gaze drops to my tented briefs when I return, and a smile plays around her soft lips.

"Put one foot on the floor," I direct as I shove off my briefs and put on protection.

She slides her butt down enough to touch the floor with her right foot, as she watches me. Appearing enthralled, she reaches for my cock.

"That's right, sweetheart. You want a ride on my dick?"

"Mm hmm," she hums, nearly making me come when she tightens her grip and pulls me toward her entrance.

I steady her with a hand behind her back as I slide the head of my cock through her juices. "Same rule as last night. You want me to stop or slow down, just say so."

She drags her lower lip between her teeth and nods.

"You're beautiful," I murmur as I press the head of my cock against her entrance. The soft flesh gives, and she takes me in.

I hook my hand under her left knee to pull it up, so I can get a better angle to drive into her. The position is perfect. I sink into her and bottom out, then ease back and give it to her again.

"*Da...da,*" she chants. I love how she reverts to Russian when she's excited. It's so damn cute.

I keep the tempo slow and steady, glorying in how easy this is. Even when it's hard, it's still easy. Nadia and I seem to know each other on a deeper level than two people who just started hanging out. We know each other on a soul level. But even our bodies seem to know each other. Because with Nadia, I understand the term, "making love."

Even this round, which on the surface seems like base fucking, is an act of honoring. Of pleasuring each other with total freedom–an unfettered gifting and receiving.

And then I can't keep to the slower pace. Energy builds at the base of my spine, and I speed up, hooking my arm behind her back, so she can arch over it, her lips parted with her moans, her eyes looking skyward.

"*Oy…*oh…*oy!*" she cries.

I fuck her harder, slamming in and out at a frenetic pace. "Yes, Nadia…*yeah!*" I exclaim. I slow down to drive in deeper, thrusting like my life depended on getting deeper, grinding my loins over her clit with each savage instroke.

"Please…*pozhaluysta*…yes!"

Her cries, her satisfaction, brings on my orgasm, and I beat into her, harder and faster until my balls draw up tight, and I have to release.

"I'm going to come," I grunt.

"Come!" she screams. "Please, Flynn! I'm ready."

I wring both of our orgasms out with powerful thrusts that end with me buried deep and both her legs wrapped tightly behind my back.

YA tebya lyublyu, she murmurs against my shoulder.

"What?" I ask.

"Oh. Nothing. I said it was good. So good."

She's lying. I make a point of trying to memorize the syllables she uttered, but my brain is so scrambled, I'm not sure I get it right. It was something like, "yeah, tibaya blue." Maybe Oleg can translate it for me.

No matter. Nadia is in my arms, and it feels so right. I

carry her like that into my shower where we take the time to wash every inch of each other, exploring all our edges and curves. Hard places and soft.

This is love. This is meaning. This is the way I was supposed to feel every time I shared my body with a woman. But I never knew it until now.

~

NADIA

After Flynn takes me to a corner bakery for breakfast—where I was absolutely fine—we return to his place. I sketch designs for the burlesque dancers on a pad of paper he found for me while he composes music.

Like last night, it's more than comfortable. There's an ease between us. A familiarity. Like we've been together in past lifetimes, so we just settle right in like it's old times.

I don't ever want this to end.

Gospodi, I said *I love you* to Flynn when we had sex this morning! Fortunately, I said it in Russian, and he didn't understand me.

I now realize why everyone was so afraid I would get hurt. It's not that Flynn would hurt me. But I'll hurt myself.

I have hurt myself.

Because now that I've tasted Flynn, now that I've been the focus of his attention, the recipient of his talents, now that I've basked in the glow he casts, I don't ever want to leave it.

Flynn puts his guitar down and picks up a notebook. He sprawls sideways in an armchair, his long legs extending over the armrest, far beyond the confines of the furniture. He holds the notebook on his knees and a pencil between his fingers. When he glances up at me, he catches me watching him.

Instead of reacting, he just looks steadily back at me, his brown eyes seeming to see deep into the depths of my soul.

That look alone makes me want to swear my undying love to him again. In English this time.

But I know that would be foolish. He's not mine to keep.

After a moment, his gaze drops, and he writes something on his paper.

"Are you writing a song?" I ask. For some reason, my pulse quickens.

He nods, his gaze lifting to mine again.

"Is it…" I can't finish the question. It seems way too assuming. Of course, it's not about me! Only a delusional middle-schooler would think such a thing.

"About you," he answers, stealing my breath.

I want to run over and look over his shoulder, but that would disturb his process. He's in the creative flow. I happen to be his muse. Even if I think it's about me, even though I desperately want to assign all kinds of crazy meanings to this—it's not. Artists are inspired by whatever is around them, and I'm the one who happens to be around him right now.

Instead, I force myself to look back at my own drawings. To borrow his creative energy and get in the flow myself.

I sketched the most beautiful corsets, tie-dyed in shades of red and wine, trimmed in black velvet, of course. The bottoms would match but the cut would vary—one dancer could wear short shorts with ruffles on the ass, another could be in a short, poufy skirt, one a long, ankle-length skirt with crinoline underneath, then another with pants.

I can't wait to take measurements and get started.

Flynn picks up the guitar again, plays the tune he'd been working on before, then returns to his notebook.

I rearrange myself on the sofa, turning sideways to put my feet up and just watch Flynn at work. He's so beautiful. I could live stream him again, so his fans can see him, but this time I want him all for myself. Instead, I unzip my jeans and slip my hand inside to touch myself.

I haven't masturbated since my trauma. Not once.

But everything feels different now. I'm a sexual being. Flynn helped return that to me. So did the Black Velvet burlesque dancers.

I'm not afraid of the past swallowing me up any more. I can let it stay in the past. I stroke my fingers inside my panties to just feel my damp folds. As I touch they grow wetter. I think of the way Flynn fucked me against this couch this morning and wetness coats my fingers.

Flynn glances up. "Fuck." He tosses the notebook and pencil on the coffee table and gets up. "Do you need some attention, Peaches?"

"Yes." I draw out the syllable.

Oh my God. I'm flirty. It's so fun.

He drops to his knees in front of me and palms my thighs. "May I taste?"

I shake my head, and he watches my face closely.

"No?"

"I'm already primed," I tell him. It's true—I don't want his tongue between my legs. I want his cock.

He reaches for the waistband of my jeans and tugs them down and off my legs. His gaze falls hungrily on my panties. "Are you sure?"

I scramble to my feet and drop the panties then turn to kneel on the couch, holding the back of it and presenting my ass to Flynn. "Can we do it this way?"

His chuckle is dark. "We can do it any way you like,

sweetheart." He jogs to the bedroom. "I'll be right back," he calls as he goes. When he returns he drops a fistful of condoms on the coffee table and shucks his clothing.

He opens a condom and rolls it on. I don't want to think about the fact that he probably buys in bulk or how many he's already used this month.

It doesn't matter. He's with me right now. And I'm with him. And I wouldn't want to be anywhere else.

It's dumb to try protect myself against future hurt by refusing to enjoy the present. Why miss out? Because then I'll have something to miss?

I'd rather have the memory of this than no memories with Flynn at all.

I wiggle my ass for him. "I think Adrian likes to spank Kat," I say with a giggle. "Actually, I think it's probably the other way around. She must like to be spanked."

"Are you asking me to spank you, Nadia?"

Flynn is so smart.

"Maybe?"

His hand crashes down on my ass before I get embarrassed. It's sharp and surprising but not unpleasant.

It doesn't scare me or bring on bad memories. I was never spanked–that would've been far too playful for cigar man. He wasn't playful. He liked the violence. Rape. He was more into choking and holding me down and forced sex.

Flynn rubs my offended cheek. "You okay?"

"I like it," I gasp.

Flynn lets out a low curse and slaps my other cheek. "Yeah? That's good because I like doing it." He delivers two more slaps. "You look so sexy right now with my handprint on your ass." He rubs again.

I moan my appreciation. I love the way he touches me–the rough and the gentle.

He continues, warming my ass with slaps alternating with rubbing, then he slides his fingers between my legs. I separate my knees wider and arch up for him. He takes my hips and pushes them down a little lower to line the head of his cock up with my entrance. He's tall enough to enter me standing up behind me. He slides in, and I suck in a breath and moan.

"You good, Nadia?" His voice is scratchy and rough, deepened with desire. I love that I have the power to turn him on this way. To make him come undone like he was last night.

"Yes."

He slides his hand up my shirt to fondle my breast as he starts up with a slow rhythm in and out.

The spanking got me excited, and I already need more. "Faster, please," I plead.

"You need more of this cock, beautiful girl? I will give it all to you." He adjusts to put his hands on my waist, so he can plow in harder. It's a good angle. I can take him deep, despite his length, and I love the way he fills me. His balls slap against my clit, giving me extra stimulation.

I warble my approval in eager tones.

"You like that, sweetheart?" He changes his grip to hold my nape. I freeze for a moment, a slice of panic running through me. The clanging of metal bashes in my head.

Flynn is instantly on me, soothing me. "No, no, no, baby. It's just me. It's you and me. You're so safe here." He folds his torso down over mine to wrap his arms around me and kiss my neck, my jaw, between my shoulder blades. He strokes my hair, murmuring comforting words.

As quickly as it came, the panic fades. "I'm okay," I say. "*Spasibo*. It's okay."

Instead of avoiding the position that triggered me,

Flynn returns to it. "It's me, babe." He holds my nape, but his thumb and fingers massage my muscles there. "May I hold you here?"

My heart pounds, but I say, "Yes."

"You're always in charge, sweetheart. You know that, right?" He presses in and out of me again. "You say stop, I stop. You say more, I give you more. Whatever you need. We're in this together. I'm here for you."

Tears well up in my eyes–not out of tragedy but because it feels so good. Because everything he says is so right. "I'm here for you, too," I tell him. "Thank you… thank you, Flynn."

He's picked up speed again, his fingers tightening around my nape to hold me still as he pounds in harder.

I'm not scared at all. I want it. All of it. I want Flynn to find his pleasure with me–and all I register now is pleasure.

"I love it," I tell him. "I love it with you. I love it so much."

"Christ, Nadia." His fingers tighten more, and his moves grow erratic. "You're so fucking perfect." His breath rasps in and out roughly.

"I'm ready," I tell him. "You can come. I want to come with you."

"Oh God," he mutters. He puts a snap into his hips that practically lifts my knees off the couch with each shove and my breath comes out in shrieks over and over again until he roars and slams in. "I'm coming!"

As if I didn't know.

My body's already in perfect harmony with his. My inner walls tighten and spasm around his cock, milking it, squeezing it. It's got to be the best orgasm I've ever had. By far.

"Oh my God," he repeats, his hands coasting up and down my back. "You're so perfect, Nadia." Even though he's the one who did all the work, who made it work for me, he sounds grateful. Like I just gave him some huge gift.

I love you. I hear the Russian words in my head again but somehow don't speak them this time.

As he eases out and goes to the bathroom to dispose of the condom, I realize it's crazy that I've fallen in love so quickly, but I can't deny it. I'm floating on a moonbeam with this guy. Everything about him feels perfect.

Everything except for our arrangement.

And his inability to commit to a relationship.

CHAPTER 10

Flynn

When we get to the Kremlin for rehearsal, I'm feeling possessive and protective and completely unwilling to let Nadia go.

Even though I know I seem clingy and weird, I ask if she wants to come and watch.

"I would like that," she says, even though she hasn't been home in almost twenty-four hours and is still in yesterday's clothes.

She shrinks a little when she first enters the room. Ty and Lake are already there getting set up.

"Hey, Nadia," Ty says.

"Oh hey." Lake lifts his chin at her. I'm grateful for once that my friends are as chill as I am. They don't act surprised that I brought her to rehearsal or even question it.

The fact that all three of us are pretty laid back and unambitious is one of the reasons our band sort of became Story's when we asked her to join.

She's big sister to all of us. Well, Lake used to wish she

was more to him, but now that she's with Oleg, his little crush is over.

I arrange a chair for her to sit on and drop a kiss on the top of her head.

"Let me see your phone."

I hand it over without asking why.

"Is it okay if I go live on Tiktok again? I think your fans would love to see what a rehearsal looks like."

Story and Oleg walk in. "God, no, we're a mess in rehearsal," my sister says. Her hulking fiance takes a seat in the corner opposite the one Nadia took and folds his arms across his chest, looking like her bodyguard, even though she's in the safest building in Chicago, considering the security they have on this place.

Nadia flushes, but defends her idea. "You can be a mess on Tiktok. That's what it's all about. The real you. That's what people want."

"I'm down," I say. Honestly, if Nadia said she thought we should skydive off the top of the building, I would say yes just to make her happy. Whatever she wants.

Fortunately, my sister isn't shy. She makes a great lead singer because she will prance around stage in her fishnets, combat boots, and short shorts and be totally comfortable with whatever reaction she gets. Honestly, having Oleg as a grounding force is the best thing that could've happened to her because she could be as flighty as me, and I sometimes worried about someone screwing with her.

She shrugs. "Okay, I'm down, too. Just turn it off if we look like total fuck-ups, okay?"

"Okay," Nadia agrees although I'm pretty sure she plans to let it run, regardless of what happens.

She turns my phone on and props it on her knee. "Introduce yourself," she says in her beautiful, thick accent.

I shove my face up close to the screen. "Hey, I'm Flynn Taylor, and we are the Storytellers. It's our weekly rehearsal, so lower your expectations–this is where we just kind of fuck around to figure shit out." I grin and wink and back up. "You guys want to introduce yourselves??" I ask my bandmates.

Story's at the whiteboard writing down a playlist, so Lake comes over to introduce himself then Ty. When Story's done, she skips the intro, but goes to her stool in the center and waves. "I'm Story Taylor, and no, we're not married." She points between us. "I'm Flynn's big sister."

"Except I'm the big one." I look up from tuning my electric guitar to smirk.

"Yes, he's been bigger than me since he was thirteen– the big jerk." To us, she mutters, "Counting in. Five, six– five, six, seven, eight."

Ty starts the drum beat, and I add in on our newest original song, written by Story.

We finish and she gives us a few notes, then we run it again. We play three more songs and take a break.

I've been dying to try the new song I wrote today on the electric guitar, so while they drink their water and check their phones, I start up.

"Is that new?" Story asks.

"Yeah. It's for Nadia." I glance her way, and my breath whooshes from my chest when I catch the look she gives me in return.

She positively glows. Her smile doesn't smolder, and it isn't sunny–but it's somewhere in between. Her brown eyes are warm and the gold and copper lights in her hair seem to match her energy. She looks like a goddess sitting there, just blessing us with her angelic presence.

I start over, trying out the words.

· · ·

CHAINED in the dark with the devil
He tried to eat you whole
You think you might need to settle
I know you'll have it all.

I GIVE it a low grungy sound with my voice–reminiscent of Kurt Cobain. Ty trots to the drum set and joins with a slow beat. Story freezes, watching me with wide eyes, like she's transfixed, then she grabs her guitar and starts a punk riff.

I repeat the first stanza now that I have the other instruments then cut to the bridge. I don't have words for this part yet, but it's the melody Nadia inspired last night.

"That's good," Story encourages when I fumble. "Keep going."

Lake picks up the bass and joins us.

I screw around with it a little more. "Now it goes back to the beginning." I sing the next lines.

I go back to the bridge, then to the hook.

"I don't know the words right here, yeah" I sing, and Ty and Lake laugh over the music.

I'm wrapped up in the collaborative creation process–the magic that happens when we're all vibing together to make a song. When I look back at Nadia, I see she has tears streaming down her face. Not sad tears–at least I don't think so. Her expression is serene as she listens, but her face is wet.

She's still holding my phone propped on her knee. I'd forgotten she was live streaming this whole time.

"Try the hook again–I have an idea," Story says. I start over, and she adds some bad-ass chords in the background as I sing and play the chorus.

"Yes!" I send her a grin as I continue playing. This is the advantage of working with family. Story and I have literally been raised on music together. We both learned to play guitar before we could read, and we have an insane repertoire to draw from.

This is my joy—the place I feel most at home. Most me. Is it any wonder I don't want to fuck this up by getting ambitious and then disappointed when things don't pan out the way I wanted them to?

~

NADIA

Tiktok is going crazy over the Storytellers. Even though all I'm doing is holding the phone, I'm proud to be a part of it all.

I try not to read all the comments, though, because while there's a lot of love for Flynn, the fangirls are hating on me. Hard. Especially when they figure out Flynn's writing a song for me.

The band keeps messing around, trying the song different ways until they like it. It's amazing to watch their process.

Adrian opens the door at one point and looks in. His gaze bounces on me and rests, and I picture myself through his eyes. I must seem so different because I'm totally comfortable and at home with my foot propped on the chair and the phone on my knee, watching the band play with a wide smile. He watches me for a moment then backs out and leaves without saying anything.

For once, it seems like he believes I'm okay.

I believe I'm okay.

They try the song again and when they finish, Oleg, who is normally so stoic you can't even tell if he's paying attention, sits forward and claps his hands.

I stop the live stream and grin at him. "Forty-one thousand views. You just gained three thousand new followers, and you're up twenty thousand since yesterday's stream. You're famous, Flynn Taylor."

He walks over and kisses me, and warmth floods me right down to my toes.

I show him the screen of the Tiktok, and a DM comes in from Cadence. "Oh, um, I think she private messaged you last time I live streamed, too."

He rolls his eyes and takes the phone without even opening the message. "She needs to get a clue. Desperation isn't a good look on anybody."

Lake looks over. "Who is that?"

I watch sympathy wash over Flynn's expression and remember that Lake was with Cadence at that first party. I guess she didn't see him as a viable replacement for Flynn. "Nah, it's nothing," he says, tucking his phone in his pocket and looping an arm around my shoulders. "Nadia's making us famous," he says, changing the topic.

"You can repay me by wearing my designs for your next video," I say casually, like it wouldn't be the total fulfillment of a dream for me.

"Sounds like a win-win to me," Story says, and I want to throw my arms around her in a strangle hug.

Sometimes it all feels too easy and too good to be true.

CHAPTER 11

Nadia

"Holy shit," Kat says in an awed tone as Adrian pulls up in front of Rue's Lounge the next night. There's a line of people wrapped around the building.

Two weeks ago if I'd seen that line, I would have told Adrian to turn the car around and take us back home. Crowds are definitely not my thing. But tonight the spike of adrenaline I get is not from fear. It's a total thrill.

I did this. I bounce in my seat, as carefree and childlike as a cat.

"This is from the TikTok lives I did with Flynn's phone."

Kat twists in the front seat to look at me with exaggerated astonishment and approval. "Yeah, it is!" She holds up her hand for a high five.

"Drop us off in back," I tell Adrian.

"What? You still want to go?" He sounds shocked. Who can blame him? He doesn't know I'm a new person.

"We'll go in the back door," I tell him. One week of dating the heartthrob of the Storytellers, and apparently, I think I own the place. Adrian lets us out in the parking lot, and I knock on the locked back door.

When no one answers, I pull out my phone and text Flynn to tell him we are waiting out back.

"Is that door open?" A girl calls from the line of people.

"Oh shit," Kat mutters. "No!" she calls back.

"Then why are you waiting there? Is someone going to let you in?" Two girls jog toward us in platform heels, leaving their place in line.

Blyad'.

Just what we need is to get bombed with Flynn's fangirls. I groan inwardly as they draw closer, and I realize I recognize them. Of course, it's Cadence, Flynn's recent fling and current stalker.

"Nadia?" Her tone's and mixture of surprise and dismay.

"*Privet.*" I greet her in Russian, which is rude, but I'm not that excited to see her.

They join us, clearly inviting themselves along for whatever plan we have of getting in.

"Is Flynn coming to open the door?" she asks.

"*Da.* Yes. He should be here in a minute."

If only I could get rid of them first.

She wags a finger between me and the back door. "So, are you and Flynn still hanging out?"

I nod. If I had any integrity, I would tell her that Flynn and I were friends with benefits. Nothing more. But my integrity went out the window the moment she came running over here. Now I just wanted to stake my claim on Flynn, to claim him as my boyfriend and to be claimed by him as a girlfriend.

"I think that's great," Cadence says. "Flynn is a *such* a kind soul." She's gushing. I wonder if she was pre-partying.

"He's a real caretaker. The first time we hung out"—I take this as American code for *had sex*—"I was on a bad trip."

I glance at Kat because I don't understand her words. She murmurs the Russian word for *drugs,* and I nod.

"He saw me freaking out and stayed with me until I could chill. It was *so* sweet." She nods her head for emphasis.

I hate her.

Something about her story makes my stomach knot up. It's too sickeningly familiar. Flynn is just a caretaker?

Blyad'.

He had told me about his mom—her depression. It made sense he might feel a heightened sense of responsibility for women in distress.

Gospodi, I did not want to be that for him. Not in a million years.

Yes, he saved me, but I thought…it was special. That we had a connection. Was I just another girl he thought he had to save? Is he drawn to damsels in distress?

The back door bursts open, and Flynn and his gigantic presence tumble out. "Nadia." His gaze is on me alone. He reaches out and snags my wrist. "Come in, quick. We're over capacity, and the bouncers won't let anyone else in."

"The door is open!" a girl yells from the line and suddenly hordes of them run for the door.

"Fuck." He tugs me through the door and narrows the opening. Kat slips in right behind me. "Just you two."

"Flynn, it's me!" Cadence whines urgently as he tries to shut the door in her face.

"Oh. Hey, Candice." His voice holds no enthusiasm.

"Cadence."

"Ugh. Okay, I guess you guys can come in too. But that's it. Rue will kill me. If the fire marshall shows up, you have to duck out the back." He slams the door behind them, just as the droves of girls calling his name reach the door.

I'm reminded of zombie hordes. I picture them on the other side banging on the door, smashing their faces against the metal and moaning.

I'm not just a girl he had to rescue. He genuinely seemed happy to see me.

Right?

Then I'm fully gratified because he ignores everyone else and takes my face in both hands to kiss me hard on the lips. "You did this," he says. "You little Russian genius."

"Yeah, she did," Kat celebrates.

I beam up at Flynn, desperate for another kiss. In fact...screw it. I stand on tiptoe and claim one of my own.

The boyish pirate grin he gives me afterward makes my heart flip-flop.

I don't even feel like gloating over Cadence's sour expression.

He continues to ignore everyone else. "You look hot."

Warmth rushes through me. I'm in the latest fashion—an olive babydoll dress that ends mid-thigh and has puffed, 80's sleeves, with a pair of punk black boots underneath. I made the dress myself as soon as I saw the latest runway looks, so it fits me perfectly. I'm making one for Kat in red and white gingham to go with her schoolgirl fetish.

"You want your seat by the stage?"

I nod happily.

He points to where he's already set it up, and I melt. I suddenly understand the meaning of the word *swoon*. Flynn definitely makes me swoon. I steal another kiss. "*Spasibo*."

Flynn's arms circle behind my back, and he pulls me up against his body, one hand sliding lower to grip my ass. "What does that mean?"

I hardly notice when I hear Cadence sniff and flounce off with her friend.

"Thank you."

Flynn and I have a moment. Our breath mingles. Our gazes are locked. Lips almost touching. There could be a fire in the building, and we'd never know. My heart thuds against my ribs in a happy staccato.

"Are you coming home with me tonight?" he asks in a low voice.

"Yes." There's zero hesitation for me in accepting his offer. If he asked me to go to a party, I would have said yes. If he asked me to go to Rome, I would have said yes. Or to the moon.

This is how much I changed in just one week. A door opened, and now the whole world seems available to me again. And I want to see it all with Flynn.

"Ready, boys?" Story calls out. "Nadia, Oleg will make room for you down in front if you want."

"She's staying backstage," Flynn says then shoots a questioning glance at me. "Or do you want to go out there?"

I shake my head, and he smiles and brushes his lips across mine. "Thanks for coming," he says, like it means something to him. Like he's happy to see me. Or needs me.

I was foolish to let Cadence's words get to me. I haven't imagined all that's between Flynn and me. He may be a player, and he does have a kind heart. But I'm not just like the other girls. I'm special to him. I feel sure of it.

"Give me your phone," I say.

He grins. "You're going to live stream again?"

"Yep."

He kisses me as he presses his phone into my hand. "You're the best."

I smile as I take my seat behind the curtain wing and begin another live stream.

Look out world, The Storytellers are here and ready to take you by a storm.

Flynn

I get drunk on the energy of the crowd. On having Nadia here making me believe crazy things are possible.

She seems completely at ease tonight—no signs of panic. She's still here at closing time, sitting on the edge of the stage, kicking her bad-ass lace-up boots.

The staff had a helluva time getting everyone out of here tonight, and I can tell they're all exhausted from the crowd. They want us out.

"Come here," I say, backing up to her and holding my hands out for a piggyback ride.

She laughs. "I don't need that tonight."

I twist to catch sight of her lovely face over my shoulder. "*I* need it, Peaches."

She giggles and climbs on.

I run with her on my back up to the bar where Danica is sitting in the corner waiting for Rue.

"You assholes," Danica says when I get there. "You're getting too famous. It's a pain in the ass." She gives me a grin to soften the criticism.

"Please don't kick us out, Rue. This is our home." I turn puppy eyes on Rue, who rolls hers and shakes her head.

"You need a drink?"

"Nah, I'm good. Do you want anything, Nadia?" I gently place my girl on the barstool next to Danica. I'm playing matchmaker here. Nadia wants to perform with Black Velvet. I want to help that happen.

"I'm okay, too." She sends a nervous glance at Danica.

"You should see the designs Nadia made for Black Velvet," I say. "They are sick."

"Sick?" Nadia's forehead wrinkles in confusion.

I touch my head to hers. "That means amazing."

Rue's curious gaze goes between Nadia and I, like she's seeing something unexpected. Am I different with Nadia than I am with other girls?

I must be.

The way I feel is completely different.

I'm not the kind of guy who disrespects women. It's not about finding some ass to "tap" or something lame like that. But my hookups in the past were very casual. Just hookups. Friendly. Never intense.

What I feel with Nadia is more intense.

It's real.

Raw.

Incredible.

"Really? Can I see them?" Danica asks.

Nadia blushes. "Yes, I would like to show you. I could come and take measurements?"

"Definitely."

"I loved your show," Nadia blurts. "You are all so fierce and perfect. Do you…" she swallows and darts a glance at me.

I nod my encouragement.

"Do you take understudies? Or apprentices? How does it work?"

"You want to perform?" Danica asks. "Sure. We rehearse on Monday and Thursday afternoons at four."

"Here?" Nadia looks brighter and more lovely than the moon on a clear night.

"Yes. If you're serious, come on Monday, and we'll see if we can work you into the show somewhere. Deal?"

"Oh my God." Nadia claps a hand over her mouth. "Are you serious? I'm so excited."

"Great. I might be able to put you in a group piece that we're performing at the end of the month. Sound good?"

"Yes! Great!" Nadia looks up at me, face shining.

I drop a kiss on her forehead. "See? Everything's easy around here."

"Now get your ass out, Flynn." Rue wipes down the counter with a rag. "My staff is exhausted from all your fangirls. Seriously."

"Leaving right now." I grab Nadia's hand and tug her back to the stage where Oleg already has cleared and packed all our instruments and gear. Kat and Adrian already left, apparently trusting me enough now to take care of Nadia.

"Ready to go to my place?"

"You don't want to go to a party tonight?"

Hell, no, I don't want to go to a party. I want to get Nadia naked and screaming in my bed. I need to talk to her about redefining what we are, except I'm afraid of screwing up what we have. Because what we have is working really damn well.

I raise my brows. "Do you?"

She shakes her head.

I cup the side of her face and angle it up to mine to brush my lips over hers. "Good. Because I think we need to keep practicing." I pull back a little to give her a wink. "You know, I think we're pretty good together."

She blinks at me. For some reason, I think she's holding her breath.

Did I make it sound too serious? I tried to keep it just about sex—about our agreement.

She seems to shake herself. "Yes. Lots of practice." Does she sound overly bright? Maybe I'm reading too much into it.

Anyway, she's coming home with me, and that's what really matters.

CHAPTER 12

Nadia

Three weeks later, I'm in the wings at Rue's with butterflies in my belly.

"You look incredible." Flynn strokes his hands down my sides.

I'm shivering with nerves in a blue-black bustier and full length skirt with petticoats underneath. A masquerade-style lace mask is over my eyes, and I'm wearing elbow-length black satin gloves. Tonight will be my first performance with Black Velvet Burlesque—just a small, group part, but I'm beyond excited.

"Thank you. I'm nervous."

Flynn has taken me to rehearsals twice a week with Black Velvet Burlesque, not just dropping me off, but sitting to watch them in their entirety, as if they were the most fascinating thing in the world. He's also brought me to their performances every week. There was tension the first rehearsal between me and Flynn's past lovers, but fortunately, it wore off quickly.

I'm the new fixture at the Storyteller's rehearsals and

shows, joining Oleg as part of their crew and unofficial videographer. The income from online sales of their album has tripled this month, which has everything to do with their viral Tiktok presence.

"Do you want me backstage or down in front?"

Flynn. My heart squeezes at how thoughtful he is.

He's incredible, and I'm terrified of losing him. We've plowed forward, becoming an integral part of each other's lives without ever addressing our relationship status.

I'm too afraid to talk to him about being more than his friend with benefits. Every time I think about it, I convince myself it's not necessary. We're already more than that. Flynn couldn't possibly act like more of a boyfriend to me than he already does. We're not dating other people. We don't talk about dating other people.

The only thing we don't have is a firm commitment, which at our age, isn't really necessary. I mean, it's not like I want to get married tomorrow.

So what's the point of addressing it?

Especially because my fear is that having a conversation about where we stand will be the thing that actually pushes him away. He doesn't like things to be intense or girls to be clingy.

"Go down in front," I say.

"Okay, I'm going to go stake out Oleg's spot right by the stage." He gives me that pirate smile and a panty-melting wink.

I nod. My hands are clammy, but I'm more excited than afraid. I'm in the opening number– an ensemble piece that sets the mood for the show.

As soon as Flynn disappears, Amy, one of the girls he's hooked up with before comes over.

"Flynn seems serious about you."

"What? Oh, no." I shake my head in protest.

"We're…" I can't bring myself to say *just friends*. Even knowing it could get back to Flynn if I say otherwise.

"Yeah. I've known him a long time. He's different with you. Way different."

A flush of heat runs through me, warming my cold fingers, spreading from chest to belly.

I knew it. I knew I was special. I mean, I wanted to believe it. Now someone else is saying it might be true.

A minute ago, I was slightly threatened by Amy, but she's now my best friend. I pull her into a quick happy hug.

She laughs. "Are you nervous?"

I nod. "A little. But excited. So excited."

"You're going to be great." Danica strides by in stilettos and a skirt that swishes like tail feathers. She's the absolute coolest.

"Thank you so much for letting me join you."

"We're glad to have you," she says.

I've been working on the new costumes for the company, and they're almost done. Hopefully next week, I can bring them to rehearsal. I haven't told her–or anyone in the company–about my panic attacks. I'm praying they'll be a non-issue, and I wanted them to at least give me a chance.

I haven't had one in weeks, and Flynn and I go out in public more and more often.

Of course, I still haven't dared go anywhere without him, but I feel like I maybe could. And he'll be right there in front tonight. Almost like he's right beside me.

"I'm going out," Danica says, stepping onto the stage.

The crowd is much smaller than what the Storytellers draw. People are sitting at tables talking and drinking. There's room to breathe. Nothing to set me off.

"Welcome." Danica uses a sex-goddess voice when she speaks into the mic.

The crowd–filled with what appears to be regulars–cheers.

"We're about to get started, so let me go over the rules for anyone who's new tonight. Keep your cell phones in your pockets or purses because no photography or recording is allowed. We do accept tips, but don't interrupt the performance to give them to us–we'll come out and circulate in the audience in the middle of each act. Cash is always appreciated. If you need more, there's an ATM in the back corner. It is an interactive show, so feel free to laugh, applaud and show us your appreciation but keep it respectful. This isn't a strip club, and you're not going to see our tits. Everyone clear?" She turns her head to the side to give a coquettish smile and a bat of her iridescent blue fake lashes.

The crowd cheers again in agreement.

"Then, without further ado, I present, Black Velvet Burlesque."

The music starts up, and we each come out to pose with our designated wooden chairs. I stand with my back to the audience, one foot on the seat.

The moment I take on my pose, I feel the power of it course through me. This power was what drew me to burlesque. It's owning my sexuality. Using it to tease and taunt and show that I'm the one in control.

On the music cues, we change our poses. I straddle the back of the chair, then arch over the seat and split my legs wide. Next I stand on the seat and toss an arm into the air. Six rotations of poses, and then we start to move around the stage, swapping chairs and adding more movement. It's a structured improvisation, but we've rehearsed it enough that I set my own part, so there's no panic of not knowing what to do.

Not that I feel like panicking.

On the contrary, I'm filled with power and energy. I grow more confident with each whoop and holler from the audience, especially because I hear Flynn's voice in the mix.

The next part of the dance involves us stealing the chair from another dancer–sort of a sexy musical chairs sort of thing, which gets laughs from the audience, especially when we start pulling pieces of clothing away from the other dancers in retribution.

We parade out into the audience. The sides of my skirt have been ripped away, so I'm showing flashes of my garters and black hose as I walk.

I collect one and five dollar bills from people's fingers and give each one a smile or peck on the cheek or sometimes a trailed finger over a body part with my gloved hand.

I'm saving Flynn for last, but I don't make it there.

I don't make it there because the scent of cigar smoke fills my nostrils, and my brain goes fuzzy.

Metal screams in my head. My eyes roll back. I nearly drop to the floor. Or maybe I do drop to the floor.

I don't know because I've gone completely blind. I can't breathe. It's so fucking loud.

And then Flynn is there. I can't see him–I still see nothing at all–but sense his presence all around me.

He picks me up and carries me.

And then we're outside.

The freezing Chicago air pricks my senses like a form of smelling salts. Vaguely, I become aware of the darkness. The sound of traffic. Flynn's muttered curse. I'm on my feet, propped against the brick wall.

"Let's get this open."

I realize his fingers are frantically working the laces on my corset, so I can breathe, but the idea of being stripped, of having it fall off and expose me, renews my freak-out.

"No, no, no, no." I turn and shove him away from me.

"Okay, sweetheart. I've got you." He collects me smoothly in his arms again and holds me in a tight, unmoving embrace.

There's safety here. In the stillness. The warmth of his body heat contrasts with the freezing cold air. After a few minutes, I register the steady drum of Flynn's heartbeat against my ear. I lift my head from where I'd pressed it against his shoulder and blink up at him.

"*Gospodi*. I don't even know what happened." I burst into tears. "One minute I was fine, and then...*blyad'*—I don't know."

The back door opens, and Danica pokes her head out. "Nadia? Are you okay? What happened?"

"It's all right. She just got a little faint," Flynn lies for me. "I think her corset was too tight."

I hurriedly wipe my tears and nod trying to make it look like I'm totally fine. Like I didn't just completely lose my shit. That was by far the worst episode I've had.

Was it triggered by my nerves? By performing?

Danica stands there with a hand on her hip. She doesn't believe Flynn. Of course, it doesn't make sense. But I don't want to tell her the truth. I don't want to get kicked out of the company. This is the first thing that's really caught my enthusiasm—other than Flynn—since my captivity.

"I'm so sorry," I say. "I hope I didn't ruin the piece."

"No, it was fine. I don't think anyone noticed since we were doing our audience sweep."

I wipe a fresh tear with the back of my hand. "Am I kicked out?"

"Don't be ridiculous. Of course not." She stares at me

for another moment, like she's trying to figure me out. "You're okay now?"

"Yes. Just embarrassed. Thank you."

She nods and goes back inside.

I sag against Flynn's sturdy body. I'm so glad I didn't tell Kat and Adrian or anyone else that I was performing tonight. Having them see my meltdown would've been completely demoralizing.

"*Bozhe moi.* I don't know what happened. *Did* I faint?" I ask. I can't even remember. It was like I blacked out. I don't recall what triggered it.

"No." Flynn strokes my cheek with his thumb and leans his forehead against mine. "You just froze and started hyperventilating. You looked..." he swallows.

"What?"

He shakes his head, and I know he's going to hide the truth from me.

"*Tell me,*" I say fiercely.

He glances away. "You looked scared. More than scared. You looked terrified. It scared *me*. So I picked you up and brought you out here."

I blink, stepping out of my shoes and into Flynn's for a moment.

He's a real caretaker. Cadence's words echo in my ears.

Gospodi, I don't want to do this to Flynn. Make him my caretaker. My rescuer. I wanted to be strong and in charge up on that stage tonight.

"Did...did that guy touch you? Or say something?" Flynn has an uncharacteristic edge of violence to him, almost like he's channeling Adrian's overprotectiveness.

"What guy?" I try to remember what happened before I blacked out, but I can't seem to recall anything.

What is happening to me?

"I don't know—the last guy you took money from before

you freaked out." Flynn shakes his head. "Nevermind—it doesn't matter. We don't have to talk about it."

I shiver in his arms, the cold catching up to my bare shoulders and thighs.

"Do you want to go back inside, or do you want to bail?" When my forehead scrunches, he says, "By bail, I mean leave?"

"Let's leave. Please." Fresh disappointment courses through me at the fact that I couldn't finish the dance. I hate that I'm tucking tail and running away, but the thought of going back inside turns my stomach. For some reason, I feel certain I'll go back into a full attack again if I do.

I'm so damn disappointed that my anxiety ruined my big night. Just when I was feeling so good.

"Do you want me to go grab your stuff?"

I don't need a rescuer. This isn't fair to Flynn.

"I can go in," I say, but I don't move. I'm not sure I actually can. There's something huge looming, just beyond my conscious mind, waiting to attack.

Flynn sees my hesitation. "You can wait in the van. I'll turn it on so it gets warm." He guides me into the parking lot with an arm around my shoulder. He opens up my side of the van and helps me in, then walks around to the driver's side and turns it on. "I'll be right back, Peaches. Lock the doors, okay?"

It's a strange thing to say—Flynn doesn't usually caution me about safety. I snap the locks down as the grating of metal grinds and clangs in my ears. Tears prick my eyes, and my chest balloons with air I can't swallow or exhale.

The sense of peril returns as I watch Flynn jog back into Rue's.

I'm not in danger. I'm not in danger. I'm totally safe right now.

My therapist explained to me that our bodies respond to immediate threat with either fight, flight, freeze or fawn.

I happen to freeze.

She explained my body now carries the memory of my trauma, and the same response gets triggered even though I'm no longer in danger.

I rock back and forth in my seat, trying to push back the panic threatening to overtake me.

Maybe I'm not safe here. Why did Flynn tell me to lock the doors?

The memory of being grabbed from the parking lot at work flashes in my mind to the sound of chains rattling.

Oh God. Chains. The cuffs. The collar. The leash.

Flynn returns and starts up the van. "My place?" he asks.

I force myself to nod.

"Flynn," I choke. "I smelled cigar smoke."

"I'm not following."

"Tonight at the show. That's what set me off. It was the same smell as–"

"Oh fuck." Flynn seems to understand. "The smell triggered your fear response or something."

"Exactly." My belly shudders in on a breath. "Do you think–" I can barely speak the possibility. "What if it was him?"

Flynn looks over at me, brows dipped. "I doubt it was," he says. "I mean, *was* it? Would you recognize him?"

For some reason, I can't dredge up the memory of his face–it's hidden in the shadows of my mind. I just have the idea of a sneer. It was just the smell.

I shake my head. "I don't know."

But I don't want to make this Flynn's problem. He shouldn't be my rescuer. Neither should Adrian. I'm strong.

I got up on that stage tonight and danced. I'm reclaiming my sexuality.

"I'm sorry. I'm okay now," I lie.

I'm not going to be crazy with Flynn. He's the guy who makes me feel normal. Or at least semi-normal.

I'm not going to make him take on my burdens for me. It isn't fair.

∼

NADIA

I wake in the middle of the night in a full panic attack. I can't breathe. The clanging of metal surrounds me. Cigar smoke burns my nostrils.

I claw my way to sitting but don't know where I am. Not until I hear Flynn's sleepy voice. "Nadia?"

Flynn.

I'm in his bedroom. Tears prick my eyes as my breath gradually wheezes in.

"Was it the cigar guy?"

I'm so grateful at the matter-of-fact way Flynn asks the question. Bringing it out of the shadows and into the light.

"Yeah." I recall the pieces of the dream. Cigar man was on top of me, choking me with the choke chain dog leash.

Flynn hands me a bottle of water next to the bed, and I take a drink.

"I thought I was going to die. I wished I was dead."

"In the dream or when it really happened?"

"I don't know. Both, I think."

Flynn swings his long legs off the bed and gets up.

"Where are you going?" Flynn is sweet about letting me keep a light on when we sleep, but even with it on, I don't want him to leave me. The fear from the dream is still coursing through my body.

"I'm gonna get us some ice cream. Because ice cream makes everything better." Flynn pads off to the kitchen, and I pull the covers up to my chin, a faint smile tugging at my lips.

He returns with a pint of Ben & Jerry's Cherry Garcia ice cream and two spoons and climbs back into the bed.

And just like that, Flynn makes the ugliest parts of my life bearable again. Almost pleasurable even.

Because Cherry Garcia ice cream is unbelievably good, especially when it's shared in Flynn Taylor's bed.

Cigar guy no longer had me as firmly in his grip because now I had something to distract myself with. Ice cream and Flynn.

CHAPTER 13

Nadia

Sunday we stay in bed until late afternoon. My body is sore and raw in all the right places. I haven't felt this comfortable being naked or even being in my own skin since before my abduction. Actually, ever.

Something about Flynn just allows me to let down my guard. To feel free. Like anything's possible.

Flynn gained another fifty thousand followers since last night's show. The short clips I posted seem to be going viral.

Flynn's phone dings with an incoming text, and he picks it up and looks at it. "Hey, this is my dad," he says, leaning up on an elbow. "He wants to know if I can fill in with his band in an hour."

"Yes! I want to see his band. With you playing. May I come?"

Flynn's grin is lazy. It makes my heart lurch. "Well, yeah. I was sort of asking you if it was okay if I played. I mean–I didn't know how long you were going to hang out."

"Oh!"

Gospodi, have I stayed too long? Is this getting too intense for him? I don't want to be like that horrible Cadence.

I crawl off the bed. "I can go now. It's okay."

Flynn grabs my ankle and tugs me back. "Whoa. Where are you going? Hang on. I don't want you to go."

"You don't?" I try not to sound as happy and hopeful as I feel.

I think we're pretty good together.

That was what he said once, but I didn't know whether he meant in bed or as a couple.

Probably not as a couple because that's not what we are.

He crawls over me. His long bangs hang across his right eye. He's beautiful in the morning sun. Magnificent, really.

I wish I could capture this moment for his fans.

Not for me. I don't get to hold onto him. To this.

He straddles my waist and pins my wrists beside my head. Because it's Flynn and his touch is gentle, nothing about the situation reminds me of captivity.

"Peaches, I have a bone to pick with you."

"What does this mean?" I don't understand the English turn of phrase.

"It means I have a complaint to lodge."

"Oh." My heart rate picks up speed. I'm already upset before I've even heard why he's mad at me.

"I'm getting tired of you not making demands of me."

I blink. Try to comprehend his words. Blink some more. "What?"

"I just invited you to weigh in on what we do tonight, and you try to bail on me."

Bail. I remember this word. He means *leave.*

A warm flush washes over my skin, creeping across my chest and up my neck to my face. Do I understand him correctly? Is he saying I have...*rights* to him? To his time? His life?

"I know I don't seem like the most dependable guy. Before I met you, I used to party five nights a week. I slept around. I didn't try too hard at much of anything. So I get it if you don't think I can man up and be held accountable."

"Wait. That's not true. That's not true at all. I don't think any of those things about you, Flynn."

Pain lances through my heart at hearing how he sees himself. Have I contributed to that self-image? I don't understand how.

He shrugs. "You can ask more of me, Nadia. I mean, if you want."

My lips part, but I don't know what to say.

What is he offering me? To be my boyfriend?

"I want that," he says.

"I don't understand," I confess. I think it's less a language barrier than Flynn not being completely clear.

He looks down at me with those warm brown eyes. "Do you want more?"

Caught between rushing to assure him that everything he's given me is more than enough and wanting to beg for it all–the full Flynn package of moving in together, buying dishes and using matching toothbrushes–I end up with my mouth open and no words at all coming out.

In that moment, I watch something shut down behind Flynn's eyes. "It's cool," he says, releasing my wrists. "I like what we have." He climbs off me.

"Wait!" I grab his shoulders, but to my distress, he keeps moving.

I leap onto his back, wrapping my arms around his

neck and my legs around his waist, so he's carrying me when he stands.

He laughs, my weight pulling us both toppling backward to the bed.

"Like this?" I ask. "Can I demand piggyback rides?"

He frees himself of my hold and flips around, tickling me. I scream and giggle, pushing his hands away. "I'd be pissed if you didn't." I love the deep rumble of his voice.

"Can I demand spankings?" I must be channeling Kat, but I want the playfulness she and Adrian have. That ease and bond they have with each other.

Flynn flips me to my belly and lands a few choice slaps on my ass. "Always. You have the perfect ass for spanking."

I try to think what else to demand of Flynn. I'm still not sure what he wants from me, all I know is I desperately want to give it to him. Everything he desires.

"I want my song."

Flynn rolls me onto my back. "You're getting your song, sweetheart. I've been working on it, but it's not ready yet." He leans over and kisses me.

"I'm going to make demands all day long, Flynn Taylor. You'll be sorry you asked."

He doesn't look sorry, though. He looks far more content than he did a few minutes ago. "So tell me what you want to do this afternoon."

Oh.

My pulse races when I finally get the gist of what he's asking of me. He's saying I get to weigh in on his time. His plans. His life.

Is he really giving this to me?

I draw a breath and sit up, facing him. We're nose to nose. "I definitely want to see you play with your dad's band."

Flynn's grin makes my whole world combust. Flames

lick the walls of his bedroom, the floor, the bed. With one simple smile, he burns down the walls between us, and I have nowhere to jump but into his waiting arms.

"Let's go, sweetheart." He hops off the bed, sending me a wink over his shoulder as he goes to his dresser to find some clothes.

I sit on the bed to watch, savoring the moment. Not wanting to share this one with Flynn's fans. No, I was keeping this incredible Flynn scene all for myself.

~

Flynn

My dad's band was playing in a microbrewery in the suburbs that caters to an upper-middle-class fifty and older crowd. The Nighthawks are a solid choice, as they play the music of that generation although it might get a little louder than the manager anticipated.

I park in the lot and unload my guitar and amp from the van. Nadia tries to take the guitar from me, but I don't let her. "You're not my pack mule, Peaches."

"What am I?" she asks.

"My muse." My girl. My inspiration. My everything.

She likes my answer.

I grasp her nape and pull her in for a kiss, breathing in her butterscotch scent. "Your job is to look beautiful and be you. Can you handle that?"

I love seeing the laughter light up her pretty face. "Yes."

"Good."

We walk in together. My dad is up on the stage, setting up the equipment with Lenny, the drummer and David, the keyboardist. I'm filling in for Jeff. My dad does a doubletake to see me with a girl. Up until now, I've been the chip off the old block when it came to women. I didn't do long term. I didn't even do short term.

I lift the amp onto the stage and set my guitar down beside it then walk around to climb the stairs and set up.

"Hey, bud. Who's your friend?"

Girlfriend. I don't know why it pisses me off that we're not using that word. I want full rights to this girl. I want to own her world as much as she owns mine.

"This is Nadia. Nadia, my dad, Shawn."

"Hey, Nadia." He tips his head my way. "You two hang out last night?"

Ugh. My stomach turns at his assumption she's nothing more than my hookup from last night.

Nadia's smile wobbles.

I lace my fingers through hers. "We hang out every night. Nadia is my muse."

There. If I'm not calling her my girlfriend, I'm going to wear the hell out the title she's letting me use.

"Your muse, eh?" My dad flashes a grin that I know looks just like mine. "Everyone needs one of those. It's nice to meet you."

"Nice to meet you," she says.

"Oh, you're Russian," he says when he hears her accent. "Like Oleg?"

"She lives in the same building as Story and Oleg. That's where we met."

"Nice. You like music?"

"I love it. Especially when Flynn plays."

"Great. You'll get to see him sing quite a bit this after-noon, too. He's going to play frontman."

"Oh good!" She claps her hands together. "I want him to play frontman more with the Storytellers, too. His fans want more of him."

My dad slides me a questioning look, and I experience

a smudge of shame over my newfound popularity. No, not shame. Guilt.

Like I shouldn't have the thing my dad wanted so badly but never quite achieved. I think he wanted to be bigger than U2. Bigger than The Rolling Stones. Like the Beatles with the screaming females throwing their panties and fainting when he went by.

He got plenty of action–don't get me wrong–that was the source of my parents' nine breakups–but never the adulation he truly craved.

I'm not sure how I even know that. He's never come out and said it specifically, but he's my dad. He's said things here and there that allowed me to piece together that his dreams were deferred. Dried up like Langston Hughes' raisin in the sun.

I know he's bitter that his bandmates never were able to write their own hits. They fell back on playing covers of other popular 80's rock songs and eventually stopped creating their own music. I suspect drugs and alcohol abuse had something to do with that. My dad's fully functional, but I've certainly seen him in as many valleys between the peaks as I've seen my mom through and all related to excessive partying.

My mom's breakdowns are just more honest. I don't think my dad has ever taken the time to look at his own baggage.

So I haven't mentioned anything to my dad about our recent success, other than telling him about the music videos we did with the skateboarding stars a few months ago. I doubt Story has told him, either.

It occurs to me that my fear of eclipsing my dad may be another one of the reasons I never tried too hard with the band.

Even now, I find myself hoping Nadia won't say more

about the fans. Or our growing success.

I look around at the setup of the stage. There are no wings on this one, it's just a semi-circle in a corner. "There's no backstage here, Peaches, but if you sit front and center, I'll sing every song just for you."

Nadia pretends to swoon which makes me laugh. "Okay. Give me your phone."

I love when she makes demands of me. I hand her my phone, knowing she's going to start posting photos, videos and live streams of me. I don't mind because it makes her happy. I think it gives her something to do, and she feels safer viewing the world through the lens of the camera, and that's fine with me.

I plug in my amp and tune the guitar, and my dad goes through the playlist. They're all classic, fun songs. The style is totally different from the Storytellers, but it's the music I was raised on, so a piece of cake for me.

The place is about one-third full, but it's still early, and the band hasn't started playing yet. I'm definitely not too proud to play to an empty bar. Hell, the Storytellers spent three years playing to however many people showed.

Nadia takes the table in front and orders a burger and fries while we finish getting set up.

We start with the Rolling Stones' "Start Me Up" with my dad on lead vocals which perks the crowd up. Nadia props my phone against her purse on the table to stream it.

We go right into Boston and then a Chicago song and some Van Halen.

I have a good time singing to Nadia, maybe showing off a little. There's a little part of me that's making fun of the oldtimer music, a little part paying homage. It's all in good spirits.

The crowd fills in, and they seem to enjoy us, which

makes my dad happy. At the end of the set, I slide into a chair beside Nadia and munch on her french fries.

"Tiktok is going crazy over you," she says with a smile.

"Yeah?"

"They love the father-son thing. And seeing you do classic rock. Your fangirls say they're on their way over to watch it live."

"Oh shit." My stomach sinks.

"What?"

How will my dad feel if my fans crash his party? This isn't going to go well. "I just...I don't want to steal my dad's thunder, you know?"

Nadia frowns. "What?"

"I mean, this is his band's gig. I don't want to make it about me."

She only looks further confused. "Flynn, your dad is so happy to have you playing with him. Do you have any idea how proud he is of you?"

I scratch my neck.

"Seriously. Did you hear the way he introduced you? He loves having you play with the band. That's why he put you on as the frontman."

"No, it's just because I'm replacing the guy who sings those songs."

She shakes her head. "You have this backward, Flynn." She hesitates. "I think maybe because of your childhood, you and Story are used to playing parents to your parents. I get it–I have an alcoholic dad."

Eons of grief stored in my cells suddenly dumps into my gut. I'm swamped with emotion. With the weight I carried as a boy of trying to parse, understand and navigate all the emotions and dynamics in our chaotic home. There was lots of love but no stability. Our parents could barely take care of their own dramas to notice ours.

Nadia must see my pain because she reaches out and covers my hand with hers. "Parents want their children to surpass them. Or they should. If they don't, then that's their problem."

Just then my dad invites himself to join us, and Nadia pulls her hand away and grabs a fry. "Are you enjoying the show?" he asks.

"I love it," Nadia says. "Flynn's fans are loving seeing him play with his dad. They're supposedly all rushing down here."

My dad's eyebrows shoot up, but he doesn't look upset. More interested. Maybe even pleased. "Who are these fans? Do you have a big following, bud?"

I shove a fry in my face.

Nadia answers for me. "They have a line wrapped around the building for their shows now. They're definitely on an upswing."

"It's thanks to Nadia's promo efforts," I say. "She's been posting videos and live streams of our performances and rehearsals."

My dad looks at Nadia with fresh appraisal. "That's brilliant." He shakes his head. "Social media has changed everything hasn't it?" He sounds just like the Gen X'er he is. "It's all about Tiktok, right? Things are so different now—you don't have to wait to be discovered. You can just make your own fame."

"Yeah."

"You guys could just stay indie and control your own futures. The pathways to success are more varied than they used to be." There's an enthusiasm in my dad I haven't seen before.

Something in me relaxes. He isn't jealous. Our success won't hurt him. Nadia was right—parents want their kids to surpass them.

168

Maybe I was the one who didn't want to surpass him. To make him less of a man or a role model or musician. I wanted to prove how his path of just playing small local gigs was the way to go. That it was enough.

But Nadia is helping me see that while it may be enough, there could be more. I could believe in something bigger. Something huge, even. It terrifies me, but at the same time, it feels possible. There for the taking if I'd just be willing to reach out and grab it.

"Yeah, staying indie would be cool," I say. It's the first time I've even considered the question of whether I'd actually choose indie or go with a major label if they both were offered. All this time, I had this idea that you had to get "discovered." Like I had to sit back and wait for someone else to come to me instead of putting myself out there. But what if being indie was an actual choice not a default? It's an interesting idea.

"You could hire Chelle's publicity firm to handle your account. I bet she has ideas of how to take your band to the next level." Nadia reaches out and wipes a smudge of ketchup from the corner of my mouth with her thumb. It's a simple gesture, yet intimate and caring. I catch her wrist and bring her hand back to kiss the back of her hand.

My dad follows it all with interest. I guess it must be weird to see me with someone I'm so connected to when I've never even brought a girl home before.

"Chelle is the one who connected you with the skateboarders?" he asks.

"Yes, she works for a big PR firm and lives in Story's building, too."

"Another Russian?"

"Russian's girlfriend."

"Sounds like a great resource." My dad nods and pushes back from the table.

As he walks away, I lean over and kiss Nadia's cheek. "You were right."

She bats her lashes with a smug tilt of her lips. "Say it again."

I kiss her again. "You were right, you were right, you were right. I'll say it all day." I get up because the band is reassembling on stage. "Any requests?"

"My song?"

"Sorry, Peaches. It's not ready. I'll play you something good, though."

We get back up and play the second set, following the set list my dad gave me. All the while, I rack my brain for a song the band would know that I can sing for Nadia. I come with a few over-the-top rock romance ballads that would be funny, like, "You're the Inspiration" by Chicago or "Every Woman in the World" by Air Supply, and I'm totally up for being cheesy, but I would love one that feels a bit more honest. And then I think of it– "I'm Gonna Be (500 Miles)" by the Proclaimers.

It's an easy song to play and has a bit more of the punk edge of The Storytellers. I'm sure my dad knows it because he used to sing it to us when we were little–with a fake Scottish accent and everything.

When we finish a rendition of "Down Under," which is supposed to be the show closer, I start plucking the riff to the song, looking over my shoulder at my dad to see if he'll recognize it. His brow furrows, so I prompt him. "Five hundred miles."

He grins and joins me, cuing the beat for the drums.

I bring my lips to mic. "This next song is for Nadia, my muse."

NADIA

Flynn gives me one of those panty-melting pirate smiles. I would love to see him without his beard. I'll bet he's even more devastating. I hold up his phone because this time, I do want to share. I want everyone out there to see Flynn sing a song for me.

"Sing it, Flynn!" someone yells, and the place erupts into cheers. I realize that, indeed, some of his fans are showing up. There are young people in the bar, and every seat is now taken. More people come through the doors every minute.

I glance in that direction, and my heart sinks. Ugh. It's Cadence again. Will that girl never stop stalking Flynn? What is her deal?

She gives me a bright, friendly wave, and I turn back to watch Flynn without acknowledging it because I'm not going to let her ruin this moment.

My song. Or a song for me.

"I would walk way more than 500 miles for her," Flynn tells the audience. "I would walk to the ends of the Earth."

My eyes burn, and I blink. Instead of looking through the screen of the phone at him, as I've been doing, I get caught in Flynn's warm brown stare as he starts the song.

I don't know it, but it has a great beat, and the lyrics make my chest balloon with emotion. Especially because he delivers every one of them straight to me, our gazes locked like we're the only ones in the room. The words aren't a declaration of love, exactly, but the song is. He's saying he'd walk to the ends of the Earth for me. That he wants to be my man.

Was this what he was trying to tell me earlier? That he wants a change in our relationship status? From friends with benefits to long-term relationship?

171

Cadence and her two friends come and pull out the chairs beside me, inviting themselves to my table.

Blyad'.

I don't care—I continue to ignore them, absorbing every second of Flynn's song to me. The meaning behind it. The energy of it.

When it's done, I hand Cadence the phone with the live stream running, jump out of my chair and rush the the stage.

The audience cheers, most of them yelling Flynn's name. Shawn looks delighted for Flynn at all the attention he garners.

Flynn grabs my face with his strumming hand, holding behind my head to pull me in for a kiss. "This is Nadia," he announces, turning me around. "She's the best."

"Thank you everyone for coming out tonight," Shawn says. "Our frontman tonight is my talented son, Flynn Taylor, of the Storytellers. Please go and see Flynn and his sister Story perform with their bandmates all over town, four days a week."

The pride in Shawn's voice is evident. I don't know why Flynn thought he might not celebrate his success, but I'm certain he was wrong.

Flynn turns off his mic and drapes an arm around my shoulders. "Did you like your song?"

I wrap my arms around him. "I loved it." I look over to see Cadence is still filming, but she wears the most sour expression imaginable. "Your fans are here," I murmur to Flynn. "Did you want to stay to hang out?"

"I'm with you. Remember the conversation we had back at my place?"

My heart flutters, and I nod.

"So if you want to stay, I stay. But it would only be because you wanted it, ya dig?"

I laugh because I often feel like Flynn speaks in riddles. I swear it's not just my English.

"Can we go? I know I created this fan frenzy, but I sort of hate it at the same time."

Flynn throws his head back and laughs. Like deep belly laugh.

"What?"

"Finally," he says.

"Finally what?"

"Finally you stake a claim on me."

I blink, my heart tripping and pitter-pattering in my chest. Then I go up on my toes and claim a kiss. "Yes. I'm claiming you." I lift the guitar strap off over his head. "I didn't think you wanted that."

"I want it. I want it with you, Peaches." He unplugs the electric guitar and puts it in its case.

"Flynn, can I talk to you for a minute?" Cadence asks.

I turn to walk back to the table, but Flynn snags my wrist to stop me.

"Sorry, Nadia and I have to run to another thing. We'll catch you later." He looks at me. "Will you grab our jackets? I'll get the amp." He makes it sound like we're in a big rush.

"It's pretty important. Can I call you? I don't think I ever got your number."

What the f? Now that Flynn's sanctioned my jealousy, I'm fully annoyed.

I grab Flynn's phone from the table, along with both our jackets, and leave money to pay my bill.

As I do, Flynn continues to shut Cadence down. "Hey, maybe you can talk to Lake about it, yeah? I'm with Nadia now."

Oof. That comment landed hard. In fact, Cadence's face turns red, and the look she sends me is full of venom.

Flynn turns his attention on me and holds out his arm. He has his amp and guitar in hand, and he tucks me against his free side. "Bye, Dad, bye guys," he calls over his shoulder as we strut out.

"Whew," he says when we get outside. "That was a close one."

I laugh. "You created that monster, you know."

"Totally. My bad. But I haven't been with anyone since you. You know that, right?"

I nod, happiness sprinkling down on me like gold and pink shimmery fairy dust. "I haven't, either," I say even though that's beyond obvious, and we both laugh.

"Come on." Flynn hustles me toward the van. "I think we need another sex re-education session, don't you?"

"Oh definitely." My internal muscles contract and release at the mere mention of it. "I plan on rewarding you for that song."

Flynn's boyish grin is pure joy.

So bright and buoyant that it lifts me from my feet, and I float all the way to the van.

CHAPTER 14

Nadia

On Thursday, I'm still at Flynn's house. I've slept there four out of seven nights this week, and it's starting to feel more like home than the Kremlin.

We're about to head over to the Kremlin for rehearsal when Flynn gets a call from his mom.

"Hey mom. *What?*"

I immediately see by the tension in his face that something's wrong.

The boyish expression he usually wears is replaced by a more haunted quality. "No, of course. Where are you? Send me the pin. Okay, I'll be right there, Mom."

"What is it?" I ask.

"My mom has been in a car accident." A deep line etches his brow as he throws on his leather jacket and grabs his keys.

I scramble to do the same.

"Is she all right?"

"Yeah. I mean, I don't know. She said she's uninjured, but she was also bawling, so I couldn't tell. I think she's just upset." He stares at his phone when her text comes in and opens the map.

"She's not that far. Do you mind coming along?"

"Of course not. Are you kidding? Flynn, it's your mom."

When we get in the van, he calls Story. "Hey, Mom got in a car accident. I'm going over there."

I hear the alarmed tones of Story's voice from the other end, and he tells her the same thing he told me about her being uninjured by upset.

"I'll keep you posted," he promises and hangs up.

A heaviness descends in the van. "Are you worried?" I ask.

"A little. But I think she's probably all right."

I chew on that. It's almost like Flynn's getting ready to match his mother's emotional level. Is this his gift for dealing with distraught women?

When we get to the site of the accident, it becomes evident that it was just a fender-bender. A cop is there taking down the info from the other party.

Flynn wraps his mother up in a silent hug, and then they just stand there together, enmeshed.

Something twists in my belly, but I'm not quite sure what it's about. Something bothers me about this scene. It's a little too familiar.

He's a caretaker—that's what Cadence had said about him.

Once more, I'm wondering if taking care of me was just something he's good at, not necessarily something that's good for him.

Maybe I'm dragging him down the way his mom is. Making him lower his energy level, dim his brightness, mute his joy for the sake of matching someone he cares about.

176

I absolutely hate the idea.

In fact, it destroys me.

I back up until my butt hits the parked van and blink back tears in my eyes. Of course, that's when his mom spots me.

"Flynn! You brought a friend."

Flynn releases her, and she hurries over to me to pick up and squeeze my gloved hand. Her eyes are red and puffy, but she's as warm as the sun. "Hi honey. I'm Monica, Flynn's mom."

"I'm Nadia."

"It's nice to meet you, sweetie. I'm sorry, I didn't mean to interrupt if you two were doing something. I just didn't want to be here alone."

"You're not alone," Flynn reassures her. And she's definitely not. She has Flynn. Ready and willing to walk 500 miles for her.

Because that's who he is. And that's amazing.

But I don't want to be *her* for him.

And I fear I am.

~

Flynn

Nadia is quiet on the drive to the Kremlin, but I can't seem to ferret out why.

We waited forty minutes with my mom until the cop finished writing her the ticket, and her car got towed, and then we dropped her at home.

"Everything okay?" I ask for the third time.

Nadia sends me a weak smile. "Yes. Your mom is sweet, and you're a good son. I can see why you and Story are such kind people."

Huh. That doesn't explain her reticence.

"But?" I prompt.

"There's no *but*!" she protests, except I'm sure there is. I keep replaying the scene trying to figure out what I fucked up, but I can't think of anything.

I park underneath the building, and we take the elevator up to the floor where we rehearse, and that's when I acknowledge that this day truly has become a clusterfuck.

Cadence is standing outside the studio with Lake, and both look deeply unhappy. Worse, they appear to be waiting for me.

"Cadence needs to talk to you," Lake says.

What. The actual. Fuck?

I seriously could throat punch Lake right now. He should be clam-jamming Cadence for me, not *bringing her to our rehearsal.*

Seriously not cool.

I reach for Nadia's hand because I swear to fuck, I already feel her slipping away. "Okay," I say with fake casualness.

"I need to talk to you alone," she says.

Nadia tries to let go of my hand. I refuse to release it.

"No, that's not cool with me. Nadia is my person"—why the fuck can I still not call her my girlfriend?—"so she stays."

Cadence's nostrils flare. She puts her hands on her hips. "Okay," she says a little too loudly. Loudly enough that everyone inside the studio can hear her next words. "I'm pregnant. I guess I'll just tell everyone at once. I'm pregnant, and it's yours."

The fuck it is.

My mother raised me better than to say the first words that come to mind. I'm sure Cadence is upset and stressed and overly emotional right now. Me being a dick won't help.

Beside me, I feel Nadia panicking, and I fear it could turn into a full-on attack.

I try to keep my voice low and calm. "Okay, I seriously doubt that. I used protection both times I was with you." I glance at my bandmate, who looks like he wants to murder me. "What about Lake?" I ask.

Nadia's fighting me for the freedom of her hand.

Fuck. Of course she doesn't want to let Cadence see her freak out. I also don't want her to leave my side. I need to be with her if she has an attack. This is my fault, and I need to fix it.

"The timing isn't right for it to be Lake's," Cadence says with full authority. "It has to be yours."

Nadia tears her hand away and whirls, dashing for the elevator.

Fuck, fuck, fuck.

"Okay, well–" I stare at Cadence then Lake. I know the right things to say here. That if it's mine, I'll take responsibility, I will support her through whatever choice she makes. Be with her all the way. But I just know this is bullshit.

I'm fucking sure of it.

"Hang on." I hold up a finger and turn and dash to the elevator, slipping through the doors right before they close.

Nadia–my sweet, sweet girl–is on her hands and knees on the floor, struggling for breath.

I want to go in hot–rush to spit out a thousand words that will take away the sting of this unfortunate turn of events. I want to promise her that this changes nothing, beg her to still be mine, but I know my own frantic energy isn't going to help her breathe.

So I drop to the floor with her. I lie on my back with my head near one of her hands, so I can see her face. I don't touch her. I don't try to say anything.

Nadia's unsuccessful attempts to inhale don't improve, but they don't get worse, either.

"It's not true. I really don't think it's true."

Nadia won't look at me—she's staring at a spot on the floor, but she nods.

"You agree? She's just freaking out because I sang you a song."

Nadia sits back on her heels and straightens her spine, some of her breath leaving with a heaved sigh. "Probably." The word sounds bitter. There are tears at the corners of her eyes. I want to brush them away, but I don't dare touch her yet.

I'm not sure how well she'd receive it.

I push up to my elbows, my feet nearly hitting the wall behind Nadia. "I'm so sorry for this. If I could go back in time and never hook up with Cadence, I would do it in a heartbeat."

The elevator dings. We're on the first floor, and the gatekeeper is standing there. When he sees us, his brows slam down, and he surges in. He's coming for me.

"Whoa, whoa." I scramble to my feet as I'm helped-hauled by a brawny bruiser of a Russian. "We're talking."

He asks her a question in Russian.

Nadia's inability to breathe returns as she makes fish-out-of-water sounds and climbs to her feet.

The elevator doors start to shut, and the gatekeeper throws out a hand to hold them open then yanks me out.

"No, no, no, no." I surge forward to jump back on before the doors shut. "Dude, you're upsetting her more. Just get the fuck off and let us talk."

Nadia holds up a hand, and for one horrible second, I think she's going to have the guy throw me out, but then she grabs a fistful of my shirt and pulls me back in and shoves the gatekeeper out.

The doors shut, and I hit the button for the top floor, but it won't go anywhere because I don't have the keycard. Nadia produces hers and pushes the button for her floor. She's still hiccuping and choking for breath, her body in a state of emergency.

"May I hold you?"

She shakes her head.

Fuck.

The elevator goes up, and she sags against the wall. "I don't need you to save me, Flynn," she says, closing her eyes like she's exhausted.

"That's not what I'm doing. What are you talking about? Hang on, Nadia. What's even happening right now?"

"You'll have to save her."

"*Her?* You mean Cadence?" My heart thuds against my chest, and the elevator suddenly feels way too hot and stuffy. I shrug out of my jacket. "Nadia, can we talk? I can't figure out what's going on in your head. I know this sucks, but I don't even think it's true. And it changes nothing between us. I mean, I don't want it to."

The elevator stops on her floor, and she gets out. I follow her, but she stops me with a hand on my chest.

"I don't want you to be my savior. I think Cadence needs you right now, and I don't. So, let's stop seeing each other."

Stop seeing each other?

Christ.

How did we get here? Color me confused as fuck. My entire world is falling apart, and I'm not even sure what I did.

"Nadia, no. I'm not trying to be your savior."

She's calmed down enough to breathe and look me in the eye.

"What made you think that?"

She reaches up to cradle my cheek.

Oh, fuck. She's definitely breaking up with me.

"Flynn, you are amazing. You have a huge heart, and you want to help everyone around you. Especially me. But I need to stand on my own. I want to be strong and not defined by what happened to me."

"Nadia." Her name comes out like I'm begging. Fuck.

"It sounds like right now you need to be kind and present for Cadence. I mean, you may have a baby who will need all your attention soon."

"No!" I shake my head. "I won't. I really don't think she's having my baby. I mean…"

"Flynn, you have to figure it out with her. And I need to figure myself out." She leans up on her tiptoes and kisses my other cheek. "*YA tebya lyublyu.*" She says those words again that I don't understand.

"Nadia," I croak. *Godammit.*

My heart isn't just breaking, it's disintegrating. Falling into dust on the floor between my feet.

"I gotta go." She turns and flees down the hall. At her apartment door, she turns and looks over her shoulder at me as she unlocks it.

I'm rooted in place, unable to move. Unable to speak.

There's an apology in her look, but I also see a steely resolve there. And that's when I realize.

It really is over.

Nadia has made up her mind, and she is strong. Nothing I say is going to fix this. Nothing I do will change it.

The first girl I want to keep is kicking me to the curb.

I seriously don't know how I will ever go on.

~

NADIA

I manage to get in my apartment and lean against the door before I start crying.

Adrian and Kat are on the sofa watching television, Kat on his lap. They both look up in alarm when they hear my strangled wail.

I hold up a hand. "It's okay. I broke up with Flynn. I don't want to talk about it." I force my leaden feet to move toward the bedroom.

"Okay," Kat says.

Adrian hits pause on the movie they're watching. "Am I going to kill him?"

I stop in my bedroom doorway and give him a hard look. A hard look tempered by a stream of tears. "It's not funny. I'm tired of your violence. *No*. You are not going to kill him. You're going to be very nice to him. Because he's the nicest guy I've ever known." With that, I burst into full-on sobs. I shut my door and throw myself on my bed.

I did the right thing. I know I did.

I don't want to be the girl Flynn has to rescue. I don't need a knight in white armor. I mean a white knight in shiny armor. Whatever. I don't need him.

I need to be my own knight. To find my own strength. To build my own life.

This past month with Flynn has been amazing, but it was never meant to last.

I asked him to be the guy to help me find my way back into life and living. Back into my body. Back into sex. He did all of that for me. But to ask him any more isn't fair. Especially when he has other people relying on him.

He already has to take care of his mom. And now Cadence and her baby. There is no way I will suck his attention from that. It wouldn't be fair. He deserves

183

someone who can give to him. Not just take. And I am a total drain on his energy.

I give myself thirty minutes to cry, and then I wipe my tears and get off the bed.

I sit at my sewing table and pick up one of the hand-dyed skirts I'm making. It's time to finish the costumes for Black Velvet Burlesque.

Flynn showed me how to live.

I'm going to keep on living.

CHAPTER 15

Flynn

In the most fucked up scene ever, Lake and I sit in Cadence's living room with her to try to figure shit out. They're both hitting the weed to get through this.

I'm stone sober.

I know better than to turn to a substance when I'm in this dark of a place. I've been around drugs and alcohol my whole life. I know how bad it can turn when you don't have your shit together. And I am about as far from having my shit together as I could possibly get.

I've been mostly catatonic on my couch for the past six days trying not to think about how much I miss Nadia. I played the shows we had booked, but it was just going through the motions and as soon as we finished our sets, I bailed.

I actually spent a lot of the time this week not thinking at all. Just blank as fuck.

The lights are on, but no one's home, as they say.

Now I sit with elbows on my knees, my head low, trying to parse all the wild energy in the room.

Apparently, Lake still wants to be with Cadence, so I guess we're pre-negotiating how this is going to work or something. He's pissed as hell at me, as if me hooking up with her before he did was some kind of violation.

I literally played wingman for him to get with her. Maybe he's just pissed it's not his. I still think it could be.

I'm the kind of guy who plays guitar–and life–by feel. And everything about this feels off.

But I'm gonna do all the things I'm supposed to do.

I rub my palms together trying to remember the last time I showered or ate. I honestly can't recall.

"So, obviously I support you whatever you want to do, Cadence." The words sound rehearsed because I'm having an out-of-body experience, like this isn't actually my life. I'm playing a part I just got handed a script for, and I don't actually relate to any of the characters in the scene.

I'm supposed to be in a different play altogether.

One that's happening across town, on Lake Shore Drive, at the Kremlin. That's where I'm supposed to be.

"What do you think you want to do, Cadence?" Lake sits beside her and takes her hand, but she pulls it away.

"I don't know." She scrapes the fingers of both hands through her thick brown hair. She's going full drama with this although I don't see any actual tears.

"Well, we should at least get to the doctor for a real test." I don't know what made me say that, but when I do, I realize I've hit on something because she kind of freaks out.

"What do you mean a real test? Don't you believe me?" Her voice is at a screech. She stands and paces away from the ratty couch that smells like stale beer and has seen too many parties. "God, I knew it would be like this!"

My next lines come easily. "Like what?" I go super

innocent. "Wanting to get you appropriate medical care?" I glance at Lake for support, but his gaze is on Cadence.

She's hot–I get it. But she's also a hot mess.

"I'll pay for the visit. Let's just go to get the facts. When you conceived. If the baby is healthy. When we can do a paternity test, if you decide to keep it."

Lake shoots me a deathray glare, but I'm watching Cadence.

She's gone pale.

"Yeah, okay. It might be too early for an appointment, but I'll call around. It might take a few weeks to get in."

Jesus. She didn't think this shit through at all. I honestly don't think she's even pregnant.

I really don't.

If she is, I know it's not mine. I'm careful. I know condoms aren't fool-proof, but my gut just tells me this is drama.

I stand. "I think we should go right now. They have walk-in pregnancy clinics. They could at least give us the run-down on what your options are and how things work, right?"

"I know how things work!" Cadence stomp-paces through her living room, still at screech level. "I Googled it, okay?"

"Come here." I make my voice coaxing and hold out my arm to her, showing the sympathy she seems to be begging for.

She comes running to me, wrapping her arms around me. Lake looks like he's going to poke a fork through my eye.

"You're so good in a crisis," she whimpers against my chest. "I knew you'd be here for me. Just like you needed to save that Russian girl. I told her you're the rescuer type."

I heard the needle-scratch on a record in my ears. What fuckery is this?

Was that why Nadia broke up with me? She thought I had a rescuer complex? My mind spins back to the night she broke up. We'd just come from my mom's car accident. Then Cadence showed up with her big reveal.

Fuck.

It must seem like I am a rescuer. But just because I'm solid in a crisis doesn't mean I seek that shit out. It's not why I'm in love with Nadia. Not even close.

I'm in love with her because...she rescued me. She opened my eyes to so much more my life could be. That I could be. She challenged me to step up and be a man instead of slinking back in the shadows afraid to even have a dream, much less go for one.

"You what now?"

She goes still, like she realizes she fucked up.

I'm not the type of guy who gets pissed easily. I consider myself pretty laid-back. Live and let live.

But right now, I am pissed as hell.

I look over the top of Cadence's head and meet Lake's gaze, and I know he finally gets it, too. This chick is trying to play us both, and I'm not having it.

"Lake and I will take you to a clinic right now," I say.

"No." She pushes away from me. "I'm a total wreck right now. I can't deal with a place like that. I'll make an appointment on my own."

"Nah, I feel like we need to get this worked out. It's a big deal, and you've been hitting the weed, which probably isn't good for the baby."

"It's okay. I Googled that, too."

"Well, it's supposedly my baby, and I need to hear it from a doctor. Let's go."

"I'm not going to a clinic."

"It will be all right. We'll take care of you." Lake picks up her coat and holds it open for her, but I know he's playing her right back now, too.

We hustle her out the door and into the van. Lake takes the passenger front seat where he slouches low and keeps scrubbing his hand over his chin. He's obviously coming to terms with the sitch. Hopefully realizing Cadence isn't the one for him.

He scrolls on his phone and gives me an address to a clinic.

"These clinics are the kind that try to talk you out of abortion," Cadence pipes up from the back. "They try to arrange families to adopt the baby or something."

"Yeah, but it's a free and an immediate test. It's a place to start." Lake is totally in my camp now.

We both know there's no baby.

"I really don't feel comfortable with this, you guys." She's working herself back up to a fever pitch. "Shouldn't it be about what *I'm* comfortable with? It's *my* body. I'm the one who's pregnant."

I stop at a red light and twist to look over my shoulder. "*Are* you, Cadence?"

Lake twists to look, too.

She gets wide, scared-rabbit eyes as she looks between the two of us.

"Well, I'm not positive. I mean–"

"There it is." Oops. Did I say that out loud?

"Did you even *take a test?*" Lake explodes. His anger has now fully redirected her way.

"No, but I'm late, and–"

"So let's go to the clinic." I'm just fucking tired at this point.

"I can do a home test. Let's pick up a home test."

189

I curse under my breath and whip a U'y to head to a pharmacy.

Twenty minutes later, we're back in her apartment, and she's talked us into waiting until tomorrow for her first morning pee, when the hormones are stronger.

I just get up and walk out.

"Okay, I'll call you!" she calls after me.

"There's no baby," I say. I don't know if I'm saying it to myself or to Lake or to her.

I think, really, I'm saying it to Nadia although it seems like our problems go beyond this situation. I knew there was a piece I was missing, but now I think I understand.

I still don't know how I'm going to fix it, though.

As I walk back out to the van, I take out my phone to try to call her then change my mind and put it back in my pocket. I need to think this through. Figure out what I can say or do that will show her that she's more than a fix-up project for me.

That she's my everything.

I need to find a way to show her that before I try to beg back into her life.

NADIA

The scent of cigar smoke fills my nose, suffocating me. The links of the chains that bind my wrists and collar my throat clang against the metal frame of the cot.

Open that pretty little Russian mouth, whore.

"*Nyet!*"

I jolt awake in bed, my heart pounding, my shirt damp with sweat.

The nightmares have gotten worse since I broke up

with Flynn. Much, much worse. So bad that I don't even want to go to sleep at night.

This time, though, the nightmare seemed clear. More like a memory and less like a dream. The edges weren't as fuzzy as usual.

And that horrific scent…it lingers in my nostrils.

This time, I saw a face. I remember his face.

I catch my breath and cover my mouth with my hand. Tears spill over my fingers. I know that face. I saw it outside the basement of the sofa factory.

I saw it last week at Rue's.

That was what triggered my attack. It wasn't just a random scent of a cigar—*it was his.*

The man who raped me night after night for months. The man I want to kill.

My heart pounds. I get up to use the bathroom and wash my face, my mind churning. I could tell Adrian. Maybe this *mudak* is a regular for burlesque night. Maybe he'll be there tomorrow night.

I missed rehearsal this past week. I spent my days in bed crying over Flynn. Every time I thought about him living his life out with Cadence and their baby, I wanted to hurl myself out the window. But it was the right choice. I made it in a moment of strength, and I wasn't going to change it in a moment of weakness. So I didn't allow myself to answer his texts or check his Tiktok to see his beautiful face.

Between my bouts of crying, I sewed the costumes, which I should have finished by tomorrow. I texted Danica early in the week to say I wasn't feeling well and didn't know whether I'd make it to the show.

I spent all week going back and forth over whether I could try to perform again—not just this week, but ever.

Doing it without Flynn there to make me feel strong seems impossible.

And yet, that's precisely why I had to end things with him. I need to stand on my own two feet.

I couldn't face them this week. I thought I might send Adrian over with the costumes but didn't think I'd be able to do much more than lock myself in my bedroom and cry my eyes dry tomorrow.

But now–I gasp and meet my own gaze in the mirror, shocked by my thoughts.

I can prove to myself how strong I am. I can take the ultimate action–enact my own vengeance.

I don't need Adrian to do it for me.

All I need is his gun.

~

Adrian

I grill a couple of steaks up on the roof for dinner Thursday night and bring them down to our apartment. Kat's in the kitchen making a salad.

Nadia has been a holy mess all week, but she refuses to talk to me or even to Kat about what happened with Flynn. I still want to kill the kid because I saw this outcome from a million miles away, but I guess it's not his fault.

Nadia broke it off with him.

"Nadia," I call. "Dinner is ready."

I'm not surprised when she doesn't answer. It just breaks my fucking heart. She's been this way before–refusing to leave the apartment, not even showering or taking care of her basic needs.

Kat and I exchange a worried glance, and I go and knock on her door.

"Nadia?"

I push it open then suck in a breath.

"Where did she go?" I call back to Kat.

"What?"

"Nadia isn't here." I check the bathroom. Look around her room.

"Flynn rehearses here on Thursdays, maybe they made up."

I grab my phone to open the tracking software Dima installed for me to track her phone.

"*Blyad'*!"

"What?" Kat asks from the kitchen.

"She left her phone here in the apartment. I can't track her."

I'm already heading out the door. "I'm going to see if the band is still rehearsing."

I try to ignore the sense of panic rising in me. I had this before, and she was just with Flynn. She was totally fine with him. Better than fine, actually. She actually bloomed this past month.

Hopefully, whatever lovers' quarrel she and Flynn has been resolved, and she's with him.

I go downstairs to the practice studio, but it's empty. The band has already gone.

Blyad'. Why don't I have Flynn's number?

Kat calls my phone and relief sweeps through me. Nadia must be back. Maybe she went out for a walk or something. I answer, but Kat's terse tone makes my fingers curl into a fist.

"Adrian. You have to come up here and see this."

"What is it?"

"Your safe is open."

I bolt back upstairs trying to make sense of it. Did someone came to kidnap Kat again? They robbed me in the process?

193

No, that's impossible. No one gets in this building who doesn't belong. Maykl makes sure of that.

A brick sinks in my stomach. So that means...Nadia opened the safe.

But why? We have plenty of money in the bank. She wouldn't need the stacks of cash I keep in there, the cash that comes in from the bratva.

I get out of the elevator and jog back to the apartment and into my bedroom, where the safe is standing open. The stacks of cash are still there.

What's missing is one of my guns. The one with a silencer.

"*Nyet.*" I stumble backward, ice and heat flushing simultaneously through my veins. "Nadia."

"What did she take?" Kat asks.

My back hits a wall. Adrenaline courses through my veins, but I don't know where to direct it. "My gun."

"Oh shit. Okay. Where would she go?"

Are we both assuming she's going to kill herself here? Fuck!

"I don't know!" I roar.

Kat rushes in to wrap her slender arms around me. "Let's ask Flynn. Maybe he knows."

I nod, grateful for the direction. "Story," I say. I don't have Flynn's number, but his sister is upstairs.

Kat comes with me to the top floor where I pound on Oleg's door.

"We're down here!" Story opens the main door to the penthouse and waves brightly.

"Flynn. I need to talk to your brother. Where is he?"

"Oh. He's at home, I think. Honestly, he's not doing great since Nadia broke up with him. He didn't come to rehearsal this afternoon. He made up an excuse about having food poisoning, which I knew was bogus."

I've closed the distance between us by now, and I hand her my phone. "Call him," I order.

Oleg appears behind her, giving me a glower for being a dick to his girl.

Flynn doesn't answer.

"Call him on your phone," I snap.

Oleg growls. His tongue was cut out, but he's fully capable of sounding threatening when he wants to.

"Please. It's very urgent. Nadia is missing."

Oleg's expression softens into concern.

Story runs for her phone and returns with it to her ear. "He didn't answer the first time, but he should pick up if I keep calling." She ends the call and tries a third time.

When I hear the low, "Whassup," from the other end, I snatch the phone from her hand.

"This is Adrian. Do you know where Nadia is?"

There's a pause, and Flynn's voice comes through more clearly. "What do you mean?"

"She's gone, and she has my gun." I can barely choke out the words. "She left her phone in the apartment. I'm afraid—" I can't say it. "Where do you think she'd go?"

There's silence for what feels like an eternity, and then Flynn snaps, *"Oh fuck!"* I hear his breath catch and release, and the sound of rustling clothing, then jingling keys.

"What?" I roar.

"I know where she is." A door slams.

"Tell me now."

"There was this guy last week." It sounds like Flynn is jogging. "He came to the burlesque show. He smelled like cigars, and the scent triggered her. Like, the worst I've seen. And then later, she wondered if he was *The Guy.*"

I instantly understand his meaning. Nadia doesn't like to talk about what happened to her, but she's said enough.

She's mentioned cigar smoke and the guy. Why in the fuck didn't she tell me she thought she saw him?

The hairs on the back of my neck stand up. "Oh." I suddenly realize Nadia isn't going to kill herself. *She's going to kill him.*

"I'm on my way," Flynn says.

"Where is it?" I shout. I'm already at the elevator, banging the button to go down. Kat's right behind me, and Story chases us both because I still have her phone.

"At Rue's. She's at Rue's. I'm close. I'll be there in fifteen."

We get on the elevator. "I'm on my way." I thrust the phone at Story just as the doors close.

CHAPTER 16

Nadia

I pace in the parking lot of Rue's. I took an Uber here. It's funny how helpless I was a month ago, and now I'm suddenly capable of anything. Leaving the apartment alone. Getting an Uber.

Even murder.

I have on my warm woolen jacket with the gun tucked in a pocket.

I would go inside, but I don't know how to explain to Danica that I'm here but not to perform. I also don't want to do the murdering *inside* Rue's. The parking lot is far more ideal, not that I have any experience with these things.

I did choose Adrian's gun with a silencer attached. I don't want to call any attention to my crime.

Of course, I don't even know if the guy will return this week.

I am sure it was him, though. One hundred percent sure.

It's freezing out–technically below freezing–but I don't

mind the cold. I actually welcome the bite of wind across my cheeks.

A couple walks through the parking lot to the front of the building. Then a car pulls into the parking lot, and I watch to see who gets out.

My stomach drops. *Gospodi*, it's him.

He came back. He's here.

I grip the gun tightly in my pocket and stride forward, right up to him. He lifts his head to see who's coming.

I don't know why I'm pissed that he doesn't recognize me.

I hold out the gun with my arm straight out in front of me and point it at his head. "Open your fucking mouth."

I already hear the clang of chains. The banging of metal cots against the walls. I catch his nasty cigar scent. A panic attack is coming on, but I can get through this. I can shoot him before it hits. All I have to do is pull the trigger.

And then he smiles.

I hadn't remembered that smile until this moment. It's pure evil. It was his expression of delight in delivering pain. He's happy to see me now, even at the business end of a pistol.

"Nadia." He sounds delighted. Like we're old friends meeting on the sidewalk.

That voice! That fucking voice.

I blink hard, but I'm blacking out. I'm going to fall to the ground. Am I already falling?

Is the ground tilting up to catch me?

I can't move. Every part of my body feels leaden.

I try to pull the trigger, but nothing happens. Vaguely, some part of my brain registers that there was a safety, and I didn't remove it first. But it's too late because the *mudak* snatches the pistol from my frozen fingers and uses it to clap me in the temple.

That's when I understand I hadn't fallen before. I couldn't have. Because the ground rushes up now to meet my face with such intensity that I'm sure I break my nose.

I can't breathe. Not even the tiniest bit. I can't scream. I can't fight back as I'm dragged behind the *mudak's* car and then lifted into the trunk.

And then I see something that flips a switch. Brings me back to life like smelling salts. Or defibrillator paddles.

It's Flynn.

He's running up behind cigar man.

I kick, and the heel of my boot hits cigar man square in the chest. It's not enough to do any damage, but it prevents him from shutting the trunk door on me and gives Flynn time to attack.

Flynn tackles him to the ground, punching his face repeatedly.

Unintelligible zombie sounds come from my lips, but at least I'm breathing. At least I can move. My temple throbs as I climb out of the trunk. The road rash on my face smarts and burns like hell.

Cigar man reaches in his pocket and produces Adrian's gun. Flynn doesn't see it.

"*Nyet!*" I lunge across his chest to stomp on his wrist.

Flynn wrestles the pistol out of his closed fingers, while cigar man tries to take the safety off.

"Give it to me." My voice shakes with rage.

Flynn hands me the pistol and punches the guy's bloodied face again. His jowls jiggle with the impact. Blood seeps from the corners of his mouth.

I figure out how to take the safety off and put my finger on the trigger. I point the gun right in the middle of the guy's forehead.

But I can't breathe. I can't move. Another attack has me firmly in its jaws.

Doesn't my body know that this will set me free? It should be helping me, not hindering.

Flynn looks over his shoulder when he hears me sucking air.

With that same remarkable calm he always brings, Flynn stands.

Cigar man immediately tries to scramble up but Flynn stomps his heavy boot down in the middle of cigar man's chest. I hear ribs crack on the impact.

The sound of a vehicle tearing into the parking lot makes me wrestle for fresh breath. We're caught. It's over now. I missed my chance.

"Come here." Flynn's voice is as soft and non-threatening as ever. He gently maneuvers me in front of him and wraps his arms around me from behind, molding his hand over mine to cover my trigger finger.

The car pulls up right beside us. I can't look at it. I can't look away from cigar man's face. That horrible sneering loathed face.

"Together?" Flynn asks. He doesn't seem to care about the car that just arrived.

I nod.

He adjusts the aim back to the middle of cigar man's forehead and pulls the trigger. The gun kicks, but it's quiet.

I let out a sob. I would fall to my knees, but Flynn is holding me up. Someone takes the gun from our hands.

It's Adrian. "I got this. Get her out of here–now."

Flynn scoops me up into his arms and carries me to the van. The beautiful, old trusty white Ford van. No vehicle has ever looked so friendly to me in my life.

He sets me down long enough to open the passenger door then helps me in, buckles me in and slams it shut.

He moves with speed and precision but also total ease. His face is relaxed and impassive.

This is the guy you want with you in an emergency. In a crisis. In a fight. But also for fun. In life.

This is a guy I was stupid to push away.

"Flynn," I choke when he climbs behind the wheel.

"I love you, Nadia."

That's what he says when he gets in the van. *I love you, Nadia.*

"You're not a project for me. Or someone I think I have to save. You have it backward. You're the one who rescued me."

He pulls away from the scene of our crime talking about love.

About loving me.

About me rescuing him.

"I love you, Flynn." I'm still weepy. Kind of a mess. I swipe the back of my hand over my eyes. "I love you so much, and this last week has been so hard."

He looks over at me—now the meaning burns in his gaze. "So fucking hard." He scrubs a hand across his trimmed beard. "Cadence isn't pregnant. That was a stupid ploy for my attention. I'm really sorry."

"What are you sorry for?" I'm still crying. "You didn't do anything. She's the nutjob."

"I'm sorry I didn't tell you sooner. What you mean to me. I just…I was afraid to fuck things up. Everything was so good with you, and I didn't want to scare you off by getting too intense."

"Too intense." I give a watery laugh. "I'm always too intense. That's why I didn't say anything to you."

He looks over at me again. "I want intense. I want that with you. You make me want to try hard in life instead of just hanging back on the sidelines. You make me want to live."

He parks in front of his apartment and throws open the door to come around to my side.

I fall into his arms when he opens my door. "You make me want to live, too," I tell him. My sobs have subsided. All I feel now are bubbles of hope. Glimmers of joy.

I wrap my legs around his waist, and he carries me to the door. "I love you," I say. "*YA tebya lyublyu.*"

"What does that mean?" he asks.

I smile. "It means *I love you.*"

He throws his head back. "Aw, fuck."

"What?"

"You were telling me that all along. I should've said it first."

I laugh because it's a silly thing to lament.

He unlocks the front door, and we take the steps up to his apartment. "Are we back together?" he asks.

"*Da.* Definitely. I mean, I want to be."

He stops at his door and catches my face in his hands. "I want to be, too." He kisses me like I'm his bride, and it's our wedding day—a kiss full of promise, loaded with love.

The kind I never, ever want to recover from.

Then he pushes open the door, pulling out his phone as we walk in. "I'm texting your brother to tell him where we are and not to bother us," he says.

"Good plan," I say.

I see the smile slip a bit from his face, probably as he remembers what we just did.

"I'm sorry you had to help me."

"I'm not," he says fiercely. "I'm not sorry at all."

"Adrian is a cleaner. That's what he does for the bratva. He'll take care of everything."

Flynn draws a breath and lets it out. "That's good. I'd go to prison for you, but I'd rather not."

"Yeah, I'd rather not, too."

He tips his head toward the bedroom. "Can I show you how I'd prefer to impress you?"

I laugh and pretend-race to the bedroom. "I'm already impressed."

When we reach the bed, he catches my hands and pulls them both to his mouth to kiss. "I'm the one who's impressed. Nadia–you're free now. You're standing on your own. I'm just here to admire you."

I reach up to kiss him. "You're the one who got me here."

"No." He stops my lips. "You got yourself here. It's all you, Peaches."

I unbutton his jeans. "No, you."

He laughs and divests me of my jacket. "No, you."

"You."

"You."

Piece by piece, we strip each other of clothing, and Flynn maneuvers me to sit on the bed and pushes my knees wide, dropping to the floor between them. He licks into me, parting my flesh with the tip of his tongue, circling my most sensitive parts.

I manage to stay present, not allowing my mind to associate anything from my past with this moment now. Not allowing the ugliness back in the parking lot to crowd in this room.

This is a space for Flynn and me. Just the two of us. And right now he's showing me just how capable he is at bringing my body to life. Heat rushes between my legs. My internal muscles squeeze and lift. He penetrates me with his tongue, uses the tip of his nose against my clit.

I catch the back of his head and urge him to my clit, and he sucks there as he slides two fingers inside me. I come almost immediately, but I want more. I want the real thing.

"Flynn." I push him away and crawl back on the bed. "Please."

He climbs over me with a condom in hand, his brown eyes dark with desire. "Fuck, I missed you, Nadia." He drops kisses across my collar bone and into the hollow of my throat. He kisses down between my breasts, then latches on to one nipple, sucking hard enough to wring another mini orgasm out of me.

Then he's inside me, moving with a rhythm we find together. The kind of motion where I can't tell where his body stops and mine starts. We're one unit, riding into the sunset together.

It's perfection.

Glory.

It's power and love.

When it becomes too much for me—when I need to have it all wholly and completely, I wrap my ankles behind his back and pull him in harder.

He braces on one hand and shoves in with force, sinking deep into me with each thrust.

"Da...*da!*" I scream and come.

Flynn picks up his rhythm and pumps another dozen times to find his own happy ending.

When he blankets my body with his, his panted breath mingling with my own, we nuzzle into each other. He slows his rhythm to an unambitious rock, and we melt into the mattress. Into the covers. Into each other.

"I love you," he murmurs, brushing my cheek with the back of his fingers.

"I love you so much, Flynn Taylor. You're everything."

"No, you," he murmurs, kissing along my cheekbone.

CHAPTER 17

Flynn

Saturday night Nadia comes with me backstage at Rue's, which has an even longer line of people waiting to get in than the past two weeks.

Nadia tries to occupy her usual spot in the wings, but I angle her toward the side stairs. "Tonight I want you in the audience. Is that cool? I have a surprise for you."

"Oh." She's nervous, understandably.

"Oleg saved you a spot right up front, and he won't let anyone touch you. Not even a bump—he promised. Look—Adrian and Kat are there, too." I point to the place just in front of the apron of the stage. There are no longer tables and chairs on Saturday nights—we pack the house too full, but Oleg, Adrian, Nikolai and Maxim have made a wall with their bodies protecting their women in front of the stage. Sasha, Kat and Chelle are there, laughing and sipping their drinks.

"Can you do it?"

Nadia gives me a little nod. I can see her mind is working hard, but I think she's going to be all right.

Showing up at Rue's after what went down that night was surreal for both of us. I don't want to say that pulling the trigger and ending a life didn't change me. It did.

But I'm not gonna overthink it, either. That guy was the lowest of the low. What he did to Nadia is unforgivable. Hell, he tried to take her back into captivity again last night! He deserved what he got.

Besides, if Nadia and I didn't pull the trigger, Adrian would have. The outcome would've been the same.

My soul is tainted now, but I would paint it a hundred shades of black if it meant freeing Nadia from the prison of her past.

Adrian texted my phone yesterday and again today to ask if Nadia was okay, but otherwise didn't say anything about what happened. Of course, he wouldn't put anything about it into a text message or even speak of it by phone, anyway.

He did come tonight, which for some reason made me feel safer about returning to the scene of our crime.

Nadia's been clammy-handed and jittery since we got here, but there's also a lightness to her that I haven't felt before. Like she truly did find freedom. Or maybe it's because we're officially a couple. I'd love to believe it's that.

Which is why I want to give her this gift tonight.

In the time between Cadence showing me the real issue between me and Nadia and ending the guy from her nightmares, I finished her song.

It became my answer to her worries.

My response to the idea she had that I was playing rescuer.

Because the opposite was true. She rescued me—wholly and truly.

I haven't had a chance to run it with the band yet, but

they know the music already–the words shouldn't change anything.

Lake and I fist-bumped when he arrived, and I thought I sensed a bit of an apology over the whole Cadence debacle, not that any of it was his fault. We both got tangled in her weird web.

Nadia heads out into the audience, and I call to the band. "You guys–come here."

We huddle up together. I missed the last rehearsal, so I still need the setlist, but I want to make a change.

"I'm going to sing Nadia's song tonight. I finished the lyrics. Are you cool?"

They all nod. It's just that easy with them. We have history and love and mad talent. This band is everything to me. I can't believe I wasn't giving it my all before.

"When do you want to go?" Story asks.

"You tell me. I missed rehearsal, so I don't know the plan."

Story thinks for a moment. "We'll put it as the fourth song, ahead of 'Remember'. We're doing all originals tonight. No covers at all. That's just what feels right."

"I trust your instincts." I put my curled hand in the center of the circle, and everyone bops it and does sparkle fingers out. "Let's do this."

We jog out on stage, and the crowd screams. My fangirls are there, screaming my name, but the crowd actually feels more diverse tonight. Like we've gained the attention of older patrons, too, not just the barely-legal fans my age.

I see middle-aged guys standing in the back, sipping their beers and watching. Then I see my dad. He's beaming at us from the back, and he gives me a thumbs up when I lift my chin.

Story does her thing–introducing us, getting the crowd

lively. We sing our first three songs, building to a nice crescendo.

"Some of you have been following our Tiktok live streams," Story says. She points toward Nadia in the front. "You have Flynn's girlfriend, Nadia, to thank for those. That's right, girls, he's taken."

There are a few boos, but also cheers, not that I'm paying attention. All I can focus on is the beaming face of Nadia, my gorgeous girlfriend.

Yep, *girlfriend.* Officially.

"You may have caught our first rehearsal of this new song a couple weeks ago. Tonight we're going to give it a debut. Flynn, take it away."

Story and I switch positions, and I take the lead mic. "I wrote this song for Nadia. *And you can tell everybody, this is your song,*" I sing in my best Elton John voice.

The crowd laughs.

"All right, here it goes." I adjust my guitar strap and start the riff, singing the words that have been playing in my head on loop all day long.

CHAINED in the dark with the devil
  He tried to eat you whole
  You think you might need to settle
  I know you'll have it all.

CUZ, you don't need saving, you don't need saving, you don't need anything.
  You're perfect in the sunlight. You're perfect in the rain.
  Girl, when I find you falling, it's always me you catch.
  You, you, you, you, you, you, you, you, you—saved me
  Yeah, you, you, you, you, you, you, you saved me from myself

You, you rescued, you rescued, you rescued me-e-e, yeah

YOU'VE BEEN to bed with a monster
   Woke up with your heart intact
   Your love is mine to foster
   I know that for a fact

BUT, you don't need saving, you don't need saving, you don't need
anything.
   You're perfect in the sunlight. You're perfect in the rain.
   Girl, when I find you falling, it's always me you catch.
   You, you, you, you, you, you, you, you, you—saved me
   Yeah, you, you, you, you, you, you, you saved me from myself
   You, you rescued, you rescued, you rescued me-e-e, yeah

I SING the song directly to Nadia, and she beams back at
me the whole time, a few tears leaking from the outer
corners of her eyes, but total pleasure in her stance and
body.

When I finish, Nadia and her friends from the Kremlin
cheer, bouncing up and down with their hands in the air. I
hold her gaze an extra moment before I back up to my
usual position.

After the set, I hop off the end of the stage to
smother her with love. I push her back against the
stage and kiss her senseless until Adrian taps on my
shoulder.

"Hey, loverboy. A word."

"Sure."

He tips his head toward the stage, and we walk out the
back door to the parking lot behind Rue's. Nikolai and

RENEE ROSE

Maxim have come with him. The three of them form a semi-circle in front of me.

"In bratva, we get tattoos to mark our crimes," Adrian says.

I nod. I'd gathered as much considering how much menacing ink they all wear.

"You honored the brotherhood when you took up arms against our enemy. You protected one of ours."

I swallow, the image of Nadia's abuser's blown brains flashing before my eyes. Yeah, I might have nightmares now over that, but I could handle it.

"If you like, you may choose a bratva marking. As honorary member of the brotherhood. You are under our protection now."

I go still. They're offering me...some form of membership? In the Russian *mafiya*? An honorary membership.

As if guessing at my hesitation, Adrian clarifies. "It does not obligate you. It is more honor. Not a true position."

I draw in a breath. My sister is already closely tied to the Chicago Bratva. I trust her life with them. And Nadia is, too. The girl I'm all in with. The one I plan to spend the rest of my life with. So yeah, why refuse their honor? Especially when it's offered by Nadia's brother, the guy who threatened to kill me on multiple occasions.

"Thank you. I'd like that."

"Good. It is done in ceremony. Next time you are at Kremlin, I will introduce you to Stepan, our tattoo artist, and he will learn your story to come up with the design."

The three men clap me on my shoulders and back. "Well done, Flynn," Nikolai says. "Are you okay?"

I nod. "I'm all right. Nadia's good. That's all that matters to me."

Adrian offers me his hand. I realize it's the first time

he's given me any sign of goodwill. I clasp it, and he squeezes it firmly and looks me in the eye. "Thank you. I won't forget what you've done."

"I'd do anything for her," I tell him.

Just then, Nadia pushes open the back door. "Everything all right?"

I reach an arm out and pull her into my side. "All good, Peaches. Your brother finally shook my hand."

Nadia kisses my cheek. "He finally sees what I know about you."

"Yeah, what's that?"

"That you're the guy for me."

Satisfaction courses through me with those words. "Say it again."

"You're the guy for me."

"One more time."

"You're the guy for me. Now come inside, there's a guy from a record label talking to Story and the guys."

EPILOGUE

NADIA

"One more time, and I think that's a wrap," the director calls out.

I dart forward to adjust the collar on Flynn's de-sleeved suit jacket, and Sasha hands a bright red lipstick to Story. "These costumes are everything," Sasha says, looking over her shoulder at me. "You are a design genius."

I flush with pleasure. We're in a studio in Los Angeles where the Storytellers are shooting several videos with a director Sasha and her actress friend, Kayla, connected us with.

Sasha and Kayla are here, which means their bratva partners, Maxim and Pavel, are here. Oleg came along for Story, of course. The band is wearing the ripped suit design concept I created for them, and they look absolutely perfect.

Sasha and I stand back, and the band starts up again. They look amazing. That scrappy-grungy hometown band look has been replaced with a more professional, already-arrived vibe.

I'd like to think my styling is part of that, but it's also their confidence level.

After a lot of discussion and advice from Ravil and Maxim, The Storytellers decided not to take the record label deal in favor of remaining indie. Chelle's public relations firm is handling their publicity. Oleg and I offered our individual savings to fund a huge advertising campaign to launch the next album, but instead they did a Kickstarter and raised over three million dollars in three weeks. Shawn, Story and Flynn's dad, was a little disappointed they didn't go with the label at first, but after the Kickstarter, he got on board with them being indie. He's now over the moon with their burgeoning success.

I take some photos of the band with my phone, zooming in on Flynn to capture the new tattoo on his shoulder. It's a peach split apart, but arranged like two halves of a heart. At the center is a single bullet.

Flynn's Tiktok fans ask about it all the time, but obviously, they'll never get the true story.

I asked about getting a bratva tattoo, but Ravil explained to me that Flynn took the mark on his soul for me, to leave me free of its stain. "You already bear scars, you don't need to carry even a drop of ink for this crime. Let Flynn have the honor. He gave you that gift."

He did. He set me free—not just with the bullet but by inviting me into his world. He's my everything.

"I hope you're going to post those on your own social media," Sasha murmurs to me.

"Should I?" I started my own Instagram and Tiktok channel to post my fashion designs, and now I'm designing burlesque costumes for six other troupes across the country. I continue to design costumes for and perform with Black Velvet Burlesque, which is my personal joy.

"Definitely," Sasha says. "Ride their success and let them ride yours. Collaboration is everything."

"Okay." I post one before I chicken out and caption it, "Sneak peek of The Storytellers new video in my designs!" I don't have as many followers as Flynn and The Story-tellers–Flynn's is at 2.5 million now!–but I have a decent following. There's already a lot of cross-over because people know I'm Flynn's girlfriend.

When they finish the last take, the director calls us over. "Nadia and Flynn, come and take a look at the rough cut we made of 'Rescued.'"

We go over to look at his phone with him. "Rescued" is the song Flynn wrote for me, so he wanted me in the video. The director wanted to go dark with it because of the lyrics. At first, I resisted–I hate that part of my life. But then I realized this video is like my performances with Black Velvet Burlesque–a taking back of my narrative.

There's some dark, shadowy shots of cuffs and chains, and me standing in the shadows, but then I emerge. Lots of scenes of me stepping out of the shadows and into the light. Gazing straight into the camera with strength. Over-coming. All of that is spliced with clips of Flynn playing alone in the studio. It's powerful. Haunting. Artsy and beautiful.

I lean against Flynn—not because I need his support—but to commune with him. To share this moment more fully.

My nightmares are fewer and far between, and I haven't had a panic attack since the night Flynn and I shot cigar man.

"It's beautiful." I brush a stray tear from my eye. "What do you think?"

"It's perfect. Like you."

"Like You."

BONUS SCENE

Maykl

Someone's knocking on the Kremlin doors. Technically, not my problem. The doors are locked—it's past business hours. It's approaching nine at night, for fuck's sake.

But I have the video feed running in my room–because I take security at the Kremlin very seriously, and this one doesn't look like she's going away.

She's hunched against the wind. The full-length woolen jacket wrapped around her is big, but it doesn't disguise how slender she appears.

She raises her gloved hand and raps on the glass. "*Pozhaluysta.*" I can't hear the word, but I see her lips form it.

Blyad'. She's Russian.

I'm up and out of my chair in a heartbeat, palming a pistol that I tuck in the waistband of my jeans. I shove my feet in a pair of boots and get on the elevator to go down to the front doors.

I see my share of crazy shit here. I saw when that band kid tried to knock the doors down a month ago to get in. I knew he was here for Nadia, and I also knew Adrian wouldn't approve, so I didn't even bother answering the door.

As it turned out, Nikolai let the kid in.

I've had to field an aggressive visitor for that *mudak*, too. Chelle, who is now his girlfriend, nearly climbed me like a tree when I tried to throw her out. I guess her brother has a gambling problem that Nikolai helped her out with.

I open the door and stare at the pale-eyed beauty looking up at me. Her eyes are ice blue, and her lashes and brows a light blonde.

She takes in my tattoos and the width of my shoulders and swallows. "I am Russian," she says in our mother tongue, ducking her head submissively. "I was told I would be welcomed here."

Fuck.

I grunt and open the door to at least let her in from the cold. "Told by whom?" I demand in Russian.

She gives a name I don't recognize.

"What do you need?"

She pulls off her winter cap, revealing a head of pale blonde hair that falls in layers to her shoulders. She's young, but I get the feeling the submissive act is just that–an act. There's a steely determination behind her eyes that makes me cautious.

"My name is Kira. I just arrived from Russia, and I need a place to stay."

***

For news about the release of The Gatekeeper, join

Renee's newsletter. If you enjoyed this book, please consider leaving a review. They make an enormous difference for indie authors.

Be sure to read the next book in the series, *The Gatekeeper*.

WANT MORE? THE GATEKEEPER

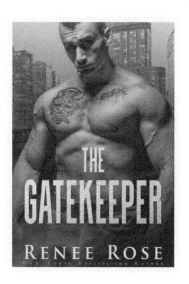

Maykl and Kira's book, The Gatekeeper, is coming soon!

WANT FREE RENEE ROSE BOOKS?

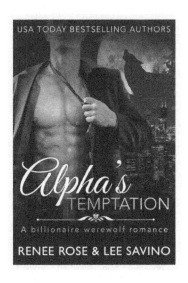

Go to http://subscribepage.com/alphastemp to sign up for Renee Rose's newsletter and receive a free copy of *Alpha's Temptation, Theirs to Protect, Owned by the Marine, Theirs to Punish, The Alpha's Punishment, Disobedience at the*

Dressmaker's and *Her Billionaire Boss*. In addition to the free stories, you will also get special pricing, exclusive previews and news of new releases.

OTHER TITLES BY RENEE ROSE

Chicago Bratva

"Prelude" in Black Light: Roulette War

The Director

The Fixer

"Owned" in Black Light: Roulette Rematch

The Enforcer

The Soldier

The Hacker

The Bookie

The Cleaner

The Player

The Gatekeeper

Alpha Mountain

Hero

Rebel

Vegas Underground Mafia Romance

King of Diamonds

Mafia Daddy

Jack of Spades

Ace of Hearts

Joker's Wild

His Queen of Clubs

Dead Man's Hand

Wild Card

Contemporary

Daddy Rules Series

Fire Daddy

Hollywood Daddy

Stepbrother Daddy

Master Me Series

Her Royal Master

Her Russian Master

Her Marine Master

Yes, Doctor

Double Doms Series

Theirs to Punish

Theirs to Protect

Holiday Feel-Good

Scoring with Santa

Saved

Other Contemporary

Black Light: Valentine Roulette

Black Light: Roulette Redux

Black Light: Celebrity Roulette

Black Light: Roulette War

Black Light: Roulette Rematch

Punishing Portia (written as Darling Adams)

The Professor's Girl

Safe in his Arms

Paranormal
Two Marks Series

Untamed

Tempted

Desired

Enticed

Wolf Ranch Series

Rough

Wild

Feral

Savage

Fierce

Ruthless

Wolf Ridge High Series

Alpha Bully

Alpha Knight

Bad Boy Alphas Series

Alpha's Temptation

Alpha's Danger

Alpha's Prize

Alpha's Challenge

Alpha's Obsession

Sci-Fi

Zandian Masters Series

His Human Slave

His Human Prisoner

Training His Human

His Human Rebel

His Human Vessel

His Mate and Master

Zandian Pet

Their Zandian Mate

His Human Possession

Zandian Brides

Night of the Zandians

Bought by the Zandians

Mastered by the Zandians

Zandian Lights

Kept by the Zandian

Claimed by the Zandian

Stolen by the Zandian

Other Sci-Fi

The Hand of Vengeance

Her Alien Masters

ABOUT RENEE ROSE

USA TODAY BESTSELLING AUTHOR RENEE ROSE loves a dominant, dirty-talking alpha hero! She's sold over two million copies of steamy romance with varying levels of kink. Her books have been featured in USA Today's *Happily Ever After* and *Popsugar*. Named Eroticon USA's Next Top Erotic Author in 2013, she has also won *Spunky and Sassy's* Favorite Sci-Fi and Anthology author, *The Romance Reviews* Best Historical Romance, and *has* hit the *USA Today* list over a dozen times with her Chicago Bratva, Bad Boy Alpha and Wolf Ranch series, as well as various anthologies.

Please follow her on Tiktok

Renee loves to connect with readers!
www.reneeroseromance.com
reneeroseauthor@gmail.com

facebook.com/reneeroseromance

twitter.com/reneeroseauthor

instagram.com/reneeroseromance

amazon.com/Renee-Rose/e/B008AS0FT0

bookbub.com/authors/renee-rose

Made in the USA
Monee, IL
31 May 2022

97294431R00134

THE
PLAYER

MY BRATVA BROTHER WILL KILL HIM IF HE TOUCHES ME.
FLYNN TAYLOR, ROCK 'N ROLL HEARTTHROB,
PLAYS FAST AND LOOSE.
HE'S WITH DIFFERENT GIRLS EVERY NIGHT.
YES, GIRLS PLURAL.
ON THE BRINK OF BECOMING NOT JUST A CHICAGO
SENSATION, BUT AN AMERICAN ICON,
HE'S EVERYTHING I SHOULD AVOID.
THEN AGAIN, MAYBE IT DOESN'T MATTER.
I'M SO DAMAGED, I'M NOT EVEN CAPABLE
OF A RELATIONSHIP.
HE MIGHT BE THE PERFECT ANTIDOTE.
THE TEMPTATION I NEED TO LURE ME BACK TO
THE SIDE OF THE LIVING.
HE COULD HELP ME GET OVER MY TRAUMA.
ATTEMPT PHYSICAL INTIMACY.
IF IT GOES WRONG—NO HARM, NO FOUL, RIGHT?
IF ONLY I CAN KEEP MY OVERPROTECTIVE BRATVA
BROTHER FROM THREATENING
TO KILL HIM IF HE EVEN TOUCHES ME...

ISBN 9798812483319

90000
9 798812 483319